MURDER

ON

CLAM
POND

DOUGLAS KIKER

RANDOM HOUSE

NEW YORK

Library of Congress Cataloging-in-Publication Data

Kiker, Douglas.
Murder on Clam Pond.

I. Title.
PS3561.I366M8   1986   813'.54   86-10184
ISBN 0-394-55763-8

Manufactured in the United States of America
4689753

DESIGNED BY JO ANNE METSCH

To Ann G., James B., Craig S.,
Douglas C. and Patrick Q.,
good kids all.

MURDER
ON
CLAM
POND

ONE

MouMou FOUND HER.

At the age of fifteen this spoiled little white poodle bitch had only one upper tooth left in her head. She was almost deaf, and she was about the size and weight of one of those half loaves of sandwich bread widows buy at the 7-Eleven.

MouMou was my wife's dog, when I had had a wife. In a way she had ended up coming with me as an unanticipated part of the divorce settlement. We were an odd couple, to say the least, sworn enemies. She wouldn't eat, what little she did eat, if I were in the same room. She spent most of her time lying curled into a tight ball on the living-room couch and whenever I walked in she would jump down and run under it and refuse to come out until I got a broom and pushed her out. When I got near her she snapped at me and growled, and when I put her outside she wouldn't return when I called.

It was cold when I put her out of the house that Tuesday morning, cold and windy, a bleak Cape Cod January day. Two or three inches of snow had fallen during the night on hard-frozen, bare ground, the sky was slate gray, heavy and soggy, and it looked as if more snow was on the way.

"Get out of here, you toothless old bitch," I yelled at the dog. She hated to go outside, especially in cold, damp weather, but if I didn't put her out regularly she would

3

wet the floor when she became excited or angry, which was just about every time she laid eyes on me. She snarled at me, eyes ablaze with hatred.

"Try it! You just try and bite me and you'll lose the one tooth you got left." I pushed her out the back door with the broom, and after five minutes had passed, pulled on my imitation L. L. Bean hunting boots and a parka and went out to get her. Her best trick was to stand motionless and glare at me when I called, then turn, show her old ass, and run away when I walked toward her.

She was standing on the back lawn, up to her belly in snow, waiting for me. "Come on now," I said and of course that was all it took. She turned and bounded away, tremendously enjoying the game, all the way to the end of the lawn, down to the edge of Clam Pond, which had a light skim of ice on its surface.

"Come on back or I'll let you stay out here and freeze your mangy ass off," I shouted, and in response she took off again, running along the shore of the saltwater pond and then through a thick line of high privet hedge onto the adjoining property. "Then freeze and go to hell and be done with it. We've played this game before," I yelled, then thought better of it and went after her through an opening I found in the hedge.

The house next door was a huge summer estate, a sprawling, gray-shingled mansion surrounded by four or five acres of well-tended grounds. One glance at it told you that a cadre of gardeners had spent days in the fall pruning, raking, mulching and dressing the yard for winter.

MouMou was standing on the back patio, sniffing at a snow-covered mound, sniffing with her left front paw raised delicately. From where I stood it looked as if she were sniffing at a big crumpled paint cloth which had been forgotten and left outside. I trudged through the snow, across

4

the yard, to the house. It wasn't a paint cloth. I had known it wouldn't be, even as I walked across the yard. It was Mrs. Drexel.

I stood, looking down at Mrs. Drexel while MouMou looked up expectantly at me, panting, her old eyes shining with excitement. I knelt and pulled up the left sleeve of Mrs. Drexel's suit jacket and took her wrist between my fingers, searching for a pulse. There was none. I had known there wouldn't be. Mrs. Drexel (I didn't know her first name then) was dead, lying facedown on her patio, her body covered with about two inches of snow. She was fully dressed in a brown tweed suit, shoes and stockings, as if she had just walked outside and lay down. Or fell. Heart attack? She was an old lady.

I needed to get to a telephone. I tried the back door which led from the living room to the patio. It was locked. I cupped my hands around my face and peered inside. The house had been trashed. A big mess, enough of one to suggest that Mrs. Drexel had not died of natural causes. And, it occurred to me, somebody might still be in there.

I reached down and picked up MouMou, and she didn't protest. She knew Mrs. Drexel was dead. Old dogs know things like that. She was shivering and so was I. Too quiet, too still. "Let's find a phone and call the cops," I said. I had no phone of my own.

You had to stand back a couple of yards to take in all of Police Chief Noah Simmons. There was fat on him, layers of it, but he was no fatso. His huge body had shape, contour, and evidence of great strength. He had huge arms and legs, light gray eyes, bright red hair and freckles all over his face. In his early thirties. He looked like a comic-book Viking warrior dressed in a policeman's winter storm uniform.

5

I had found a phone in a house about a half mile down Clam Pond Drive and, after a momentary gasp of disbelief, his instructions were swift and precise. "Go stand in the entrance of the driveway and wait for us. Don't reenter the property and don't allow anybody else to enter the property."

And that was where he found me fifteen minutes later when he arrived, leading a contingent of two squad cars and an ambulance rescue unit—four cops, two paramedics—which constituted just about the entire law force in the little Cape Cod village of North Walpole, Massachusetts, where usually nothing much happens in January.

"I'm McFarland," I told him when he got out of the squad car. "I live next door. Nobody else has been around."

He nodded in acknowledgment and gazed for a moment at the house, whose outlines were obscured by the snow. Shook his head.

"You knew her?" I asked.

"Very well. She was a good friend of mine, a dear friend. You sure she's dead, McFarland? You ever seen a dead person before?"

"Yes, I have. I was in the Marine Corps. Like I told you on the phone, I felt her pulse. She's dead. Cold. Lying facedown on the back patio. Been dead at least a couple of hours, I'd guess. Sorry, chief."

"Poor old woman. Otherwise you didn't touch her? Didn't turn her over or anything?"

"Correct."

"You didn't try to enter the house?"

"No way."

"See anybody else around?"

"No. No tracks either that I could see. I just found her and ran for the nearest phone, chief."

"Well, you strike me as a pretty smart fellow. We don't

6

know who might be inside that house, do we? Also, this usually is the point where us small-town cops rush in and destroy all the evidence, screw things up. Except in this instance we are not going to do that. *Festina lente! Semper festina lente.*"

"If you say so."

He summoned his men. "Okay, here's the drill. Let's pull both patrol cars off the road, inside the hedge. No need to attract unnecessary attention. Smith, stay at the driveway entrance. Nobody enters, nobody leaves. And get on the radio and get the M.E. over here. Bunn, walk down and search along the pond. And watch out for footprints when you cross the lawn. Appleton, go down and position yourself at the front door. Do not, repeat do not try to enter the house. Take a shotgun. Go! Paramedics, follow me in the ambulance down the drive and around the house to the back. McFarland, you come with me."

And away we went. Mrs. Drexel was still there. The paramedics, well trained, quickly examined her. Still dead, too.

"She's gone, chief," the senior man said. "I'd say she's been dead for hours."

"Okay. Don't touch her anymore. Let's wait for the medical examiner." Noah Simmons was carrying a 12-gauge Winchester automatic cradled in his arms. He snapped off the safety. "I'm going to take a look around. You three stay here." He walked over and tried the back door; still locked. Peered inside, then walked around the house, slowly, cautiously, gazing down at the ground and up at the windows as he made his way. When he returned he shrugged his big shoulders. "Nothing. No open doors, no open windows. Alarm's silent. No sign of forced entry that I can see. A mystery, that's what we seem to have on our hands here." He glanced at MouMou who was still shivering in my arms. "Why don't you take that dog home before she freezes,

Mr. McFarland? I'll be taking my time here, having a good look inside. Then I'll be paying you a visit. *Te posterius videbo*, alligator."

"Three hundred. On the nose," he said to me about an hour later, when he was taking off his parka.

"I would have said about that. There's a lot to you."

"You're no small fry yourself. What? Six-two, two-twenty? I haven't gained or lost a pound since I was twenty years old. Everybody tries to guess my weight the first time they meet me so I always tell them straight off."

"What do they call you around town? Big Red?"

"They know better. I always hated that name. When I was a kid I hated my size. Runs in the family."

"Just the same, big as you are you got to have a nickname."

"Behind my back the kids call me Big Foot. For some reason I don't mind that."

We were in my living room. We sat down before the fire and he took out a small white notebook. Obviously the time had come for him to ask me a few questions. At this point I was the only person he had to question.

"Okay, you found her, felt her pulse, then tried to go inside the house and call us. But the door was locked, right?"

"Yes. Also I thought that whoever killed her might still be inside the house. And might be armed. Look, I want as little to do with this as possible."

He leaned forward. It was like being in Alaska in the spring, watching an Arctic glacier cracking and falling, calving an iceberg. "So how did you know she'd been killed? How did you know she didn't walk outside to get a breath of fresh air, have a stroke, or fall down and break her hip and couldn't get up?"

"Because when I found the door locked I looked through a window and saw the house had been tossed. Obviously not by her."

"Well, you were right to think that way. It does look like murder, damn it. Were you ever inside that house, McFarland?"

"Yes. Once. Briefly. Yesterday morning. My dog got out and ran over to her place. She let her inside and the dog ran upstairs and got under a bed. I had to go in and push her out with a broom."

"So we'll be finding your prints probably. Did you do anything else? Sit down in a chair, for example?"

"No. Mrs. Drexel came marching down here, pounded on the door, explained the situation and ordered me to do something about it. I was ushered in and out of her house and given a running lecture for not having the dog washed and groomed."

"Sounds like her. And you're right. The house was a mess. Things thrown all over the place. Even the refrigerator."

"I know I'm sticking my nose into your business, but I have had a little experience in things like this. Don't let people who don't know what they're doing search that house."

"Nobody gets into that house without my say-so. I went through it carefully without touching a thing. I got three men posted outside. And I phoned for a forensic unit from the state crime lab in Boston. They're on their way."

"Medical examiner?"

"Come and gone. A retired professor of pathology at Harvard Med. The autopsy will be done at Hyannis, which is fine."

"And all you need now is a prime suspect. Sorry I don't qualify."

"Look, I won't beat around the bush with you. We've taken notice of you. You drifted into town a couple of weeks ago alone, checked into The Buckaneer Inn and spent the next few days cruising around in an old Ford station wagon a wholesale dealer wouldn't give you five hundred bucks for. Looking at the harbor, the fishing boats at the commercial pier, houses. In the dead of winter."

"Not against the law."

"Certainly not." He pulled a cigar from his shirt pocket and lit it. "About five bucks apiece. Except you can't get them, not in this country. Cuban. And well you might wonder how a humble small-town police chief could afford such. Well, I'll tell you. I can't. But this is a summer-resort town and there's a man from New York City who owns a big summer place here, a stockbroker, and every Labor Day he gives me two boxes of these things. Because he closes his house down in the winter, drains the pipes—padlocks, expensive alarm system, the works. And he thinks two boxes of Havanas will inspire me to make especially close inspections of his place. I take them, why not? I love a good cigar. But I don't tell him we make especially close inspections of all the summer property during the winter. Some of those places are loaded—silver, art, color televisions. That's why we took notice of you. Only natural."

"Understood."

"So next you're in the Binnacle drinking alone. Until you fall into a conversation at the bar with Matt O'Neil, the real estate man. Who drinks too much and spends too much time in the place, you ask me. It turns out you two were in the same Marine Corps battalion at the same time in Korea yet never knew one another. You had mutual friends, he tells me. You tell Matt you're new in town, just passing through, and you need shelter, and he says he handles this place and you can house-sit if you'll look after things. So here you are. Which is fine. Except, who the hell are you?"

"That's a question I've been asking myself lately, chief. Do you check out every stranger who shows up here in the winter?"

"As best we can. Not that many people show up here in the winter. And we don't have all that much to do. You keep any weapons in the house, McFarland?"

"No, I don't keep any weapons in the house."

"Understand, it's just that you're here, right next door, and a total stranger."

"I'll give you names and numbers. I'll also tell you in advance, no record. I'm clean. Sorry I can't make it that easy for you. Just an old newspaperman, out of work and down on his luck."

"Reporter? All I need."

"Unemployed if that helps any."

"I still got to check you out. So write down those names and numbers for me."

"Christ sakes, I'm an old police reporter." I gave him a list of references and got up. "I'm going to have a Bloody Mary. Want one?"

"Why not?" He looked around the room. "You are not the neatest person in the world, McFarland."

He was right. The place was a mess. It was a big, old New England summer cottage with seven bedrooms and it sat on six acres of ground which ended at the shore of Clam Pond, a saltwater inlet off Nantucket Sound. Gardeners paid regular visits in the summer to cut the grass and trim the hedges. The exterior of the house looked okay, the roof, the brick chimney, the gray shingles dotted with occasional raw, unweathered replacements, the white woodwork which had been repainted not long ago.

Inside it was a different story, clean enough but faded and worn. The house was not winterized but there was a big stone fireplace and a small gas floor furnace in the living room which really was to ward off the chill on foggy summer nights and in winter provided just enough heat to keep the water pipes from freezing. The one reliable bathroom ran hot and cold, more often cold, no matter how much you fiddled with the water heater. The upstairs bedrooms were musty and sparsely furnished. The living room where Noah Simmons and I were sitting had a worn hooked rug, old and faded chintz-covered chairs and couches, old chipped lamps, old everything. Even the bookcases were filled with old books published in the thirties and forties—Edna Ferber, Clarence Day, John P. Marquand. And when the wind blew the old house moaned and creaked. I had moved a cot into the living room, the warmest room by far, where I tried to keep a fire going round the clock. It was camping out, sure enough.

"The old Hollings place," Noah Simmons said. "You know, I've been looking at this place from the outside all my life and this is the first time I've ever been inside it. The owners haven't been here in years. They rent it out in the summer and just let it sit and weather in the winter."

I opened the front door, got a pan of ice from the steps, the ice pick from the mantel, vodka, Mr. T and glasses from the whatnot in the corner and made us two drinks. "There's an old refrigerator in the kitchen that has a coil top on it and I think it breathed its last breath a couple of days ago. So I'm using the front steps," I said, offering him his drink. "Good luck on the case."

He took a big gulp. "Every door locked, every window, and no signs of any struggle for entry. You know what that suggests?"

"That she knew the person and let him into the house herself," I said. "It doesn't make any sense."

"*Id credendum*. She knows somebody well enough to let

12

him in, yet he trashes the house. When she runs outside trying to get away from him he follows, the door closes behind them, and they're both locked out. If that's what happened."

"Which suggests that the house was trashed before they went outside."

"But what was she doing while that was happening? Sipping tea? Besides, the house looked *funny*."

"You just lost me."

"You got two basic kinds of house-trashers. Kids on a rip and pros looking for valuables. You can almost tell which kind you're dealing with by the kind of mess they make. And this mess really doesn't fit either category."

"It'll sort itself out."

"Yes. It will."

I decided I liked the guy and I believed he liked me. I'm ususally not much for making snap judgments about people—too often they prove wrong—but now and then you meet somebody and within a few minutes you know you're going to be friends. You mesh. That's how it was with Noah Simmons and me.

"Maybe it was robbery, pure and simple. Happens all the time. Don't count it out. She obviously was a rich old woman."

"Rich? You don't know rich. Jane Drexel was the only child of a very rich couple from Boston who married the only child of an even richer couple from Boston. They never had children themselves, so when her husband died, twenty years ago or so I guess, Mrs. Drexel got it all. Nobody knows how much money that old woman was worth. Millions. So rich she's got a house in Palm Beach the size of a city post office. Went down every winter in a private railroad car. Can you imagine that these days?"

"So rich, why was she up here this time of year? It's not exactly the season."

"I really don't know. You're right, it is unusual. I'm told she came here for a few days on business."

"She owned a business here?"

He snorted. "Jane Drexel *thought* she owned North Walpole. She lived here every summer and early fall since she was a girl. In the same house. This town was her hobby as much as anything."

"You mean she meddled."

"Some people called it that. But she spent a lot of money on this town over the years. She bought up land around the salt ponds and gave it to the preservation society, for example. To keep the developers out. The congregational church is run down, she pays to have it repaired and painted. And has the old clock in the steeple fixed while she's at it. And her not even a member. Lots of things like that. The village wouldn't look the same except for her."

"A lot of people must have thought highly of her."

"Some did, a few. It's funny. People here take such things for granted for some reason. Most people considered her as a rich, spoiled, headstrong old bitch. And I suppose the case could be made either way." He gazed out the window at the falling snow. "I liked her. She put me through college. Tufts. Paid for every cent of it. I was just out of high school, pumping gas at a marina and clamming early mornings and evenings, on the tide, and I'd probably still be at it except for her. And I'm not the only one."

I chipped more ice for our drinks, decided the time had come to be a bit more formal and correct. "Where do I stand, Chief Simmons? I'll cooperate in every way I can. But I really don't know anything more than I've told you."

"Just stick around and keep in touch. Like I said, I'm going to check you out. But I've got nothing to hold you on, is what I'm saying. At least not yet."

"Terrific. That gives me a great feeling of security."

"You understand my position."

"I do. But one thing puzzles me. The house was a mess, but there was no sign of a struggle. The woman you just described to me wouldn't quietly sit there."

"I said there was no sign of a struggle for entry into the house. There were plenty of signs of violence. That house reeked of it. The refrigerator, door wide open, contents scattered all over the floor."

"What does the medical examiner say?"

"Nothing yet. We agreed, get the body out of there as quick as possible. It looks like she was strangled and she probably was. We'll know more when the coroner in Barnstable does the autopsy. At least, in your defense, there's no evidence to indicate she was stabbed with a slightly rusted sharp-pointed instrument."

He looked at my ice pick. I looked at it. We looked at each other. "Lucky me," I said.

He got up, finished his drink, got his parka. "Okay. Thanks for the drink, McFarland. And *non exite urbem sine me videndo*."

"Don't leave town without checking with you. Right?"

"*Id credendum*."

You better believe it.

TWO

I SCRAMBLED MouMou AN egg for lunch, and a couple for me as well. A friend of mine, a food writer, once told me to buy only the smallest eggs available because they are the ones laid by younger hens so the yolks stand up and they taste better. For the best scramble, he said, add a dribble of cold water—never milk or cream—and one authoritative shake of Tabasco sauce for each egg, then scramble over a medium flame. And that's how I make them.

MouMou sniffed at her egg and turned away in disdain, as if she'd been offered cold Ken-L-Ration. "Eat it or starve, sweetheart," I told her. An egg was about all she would or could eat. Every night before I went to bed I always crushed half an aspirin and folded the powder into a piece of chocolate which I had warmed in a toaster oven until it was soft. She had arthritis and unless I did that the old bitch cried in the night and kept me awake.

I cut her egg into tiny bites with my fork, which is what she had been lobbying for, left her in the kitchen and walked into the living room and ate mine out of the skillet, why dirty a plate. I got the fire built up and sat down in one of the chairs closest to it to consider my present circumstances, which were not all that great.

I was all screwed up, in a prolonged personal and professional spin, nearly out of control. I had been trying to convince myself for weeks that I was just on normal down time, off the line for a little preventative maintenance, but the fact was that I seemed to have pushed some sort of permanent hold button. I was immobile. I couldn't make myself do anything, start anything. I was just sitting around in a cold house, something I had never done before in my entire life. Sitting, brooding, feeling sorry for myself.

An old woman probably had been killed the night before while I had lain tossing and turning in bed, obsessed by my own thoughts, only a couple of hundred yards away. If she had screamed for help, would I have heard her? Would it have registered in my mind? I really didn't know. *Had she screamed?* I didn't know. Now the forensic team from Boston, flown down in a helicopter, was over there with Noah Simmons, picking the house apart, dusting for prints, taking pictures, measuring, collecting and bagging for microscopic and chemical analysis. A full-fledged murder investigation was in progress and my mind was on other, faraway matters.

I sat, gazed at the fire, as I had for days and days, and thought about my wife, Earline, and all that had happened. I hate injustice, especially when I am its victim, but I decided that my reaction to what she had done to me might have been a little heavy-handed. I had acted totally out of character.

We were in the bedroom and Earline was getting ready for bed when I went off my nut. She came out of her bathroom (I used the smaller one down the hall; hers looked like a chemistry lab) stark naked, heading for her clothes closet to get a fresh nightgown.

"Time for *Dallas*. Get Channel Two, will you?" she said.

We had a new 19-inch Sony, two weeks old, perfect picture with only an inside antenna. I walked over to the set, picked it up, jerking the plug from the wall socket in the process, and threw it out the bedroom window. Which got her attention.

"What in the name of God!" Earline screamed.

MouMou was lying at the foot of the bed and she came flying at me in fury and tried to bite me on my leg. I grabbed Earline by her hair and jerked her down on the bed. She was a natural redhead and too old to wear her hair as long as she did, halfway down to her ass like a teenager. But she loved her hair. She was thirty-two.

"Mac, what's got into you?" she cried.

"I'm going to kill you," I told her. Never in my life had I been so close to losing control of myself. I was trembling.

"What is this? What's wrong with you?"

Ah, Christ! She knew. I could see it in her face.

I reached over to my bedside table. The gun I pulled out of the drawer was a .38 caliber Colt revolver a homicide detective had given me years before when I was a reporter on the police beat. We'd had pizza and beer for lunch and when we got back to his car he opened the glove compartment and pulled out a brown paper bag. "Don't ask and don't ever say I never gave you anything," he said. "And don't worry, it's clean. Sometimes in cases these things just pop up, you know? Something you ought to have around the house for self-protection in this stinking town." I had never fired the weapon. I sat with it now in my hand, the safety off.

"Now you sit there, Earline. You just sit there. Don't move," I said. "And don't talk. Not one word. You understand me? Nod your head yes." She did.

"You are dumb," I told her. "You think you're smart, but you're not. Not even street-smart. You're a know-it-all, think you know everything when you don't know shit. You're stupid. Aren't you? Nod your head yes." She did.

18

"You're dumb and you're vulgar. You wear your hair too long for somebody your age. Your heels are too high, like spikes. Your dresses are too tight and too bright. You walk out of here every morning to go to work and you look like a hooker. You look like a hooker, don't you?" This time she nodded her head yes without being ordered to do it.

"Okay, now let's get down to business here. You and I have lots of serious business to take care of," I said. I reached into the drawer of my bedside table again and pulled out the little red book and tossed it to her. "I came across this by accident. You can say two words to me."

What did I expect her to say? *I'm sorry?* Her name told you a lot. She was the only child of some asshole named Earl who had wanted a son. And despite her clear miss at good taste she truly was a good-looking woman with a beautiful body and an enormous sexual appetite. One good, long night with Earline and the next morning you felt like a chicken that had been run over by a Mack truck.

We had been married less than three years, no kids and a mismatch from the word go. Those things just happen, I guess. Hell, half the married people I know are mismatched, or seem that way to me.

For one thing, I had never been married before and by the time I met Earline I guess I had waited too long and grown too weary of slick, smart women. Hard to admit, but true. I mistook Earline's stupidity for naivete, which I found charming and refreshing at first, and her vulgarity for earthiness, which I found sexy.

I don't know. I just did it. A basic mistake. Happens a lot. Still, two people live together, eat and sleep together, spend all that time together, screw and worry about bills, clean the yard and buy food at the supermarket together, go to parties, celebrate holidays, take care of each other when you get sick, laugh at the good television sitcoms, etc. Do all that over two or three years and you get close. And something very close to love comes to exist. At least it had for me. Trust? Friendship? A common bond forged by time? Name it; she broke my heart. Heart broken by a slut.

"Two words," I said again.

"Fuck you."

I stuck the barrel of the pistol in her face. Was this *me* doing this? "The safety's off so don't mess around with me. Just read me the red book. Read it slowly. You dumbass."

She was a dental technician, and a good one. She cleaned teeth—I had met her when she cleaned mine—and now she had fallen for the dentist she worked for. That's all, an office romance, happens every day. The red book was very steamy, a diary in which she had recorded the details of the sexual shoot-out she had been having with Les, the dentist. That's how obtuse Earline was, to screw around, then leave a record of it all in the unlocked drawer of her night table.

I had found the diary that afternoon entirely by accident when I was searching around for a misplaced key. I had no idea she was keeping a diary and simple curiosity made me sneak a look, which I know is not an honorable thing to do. Invasion of privacy and all that. But I hadn't suspected infidelity, wasn't compelled by jealousy. I just got a kick out of Earline's spelling. But the impulse backfired in my face.

Les was a music freak who had a classical Muzak channel piped into his office so he could hum along to the Mozart while he tightened the braces on the teeth of terrified children. He was also a physical fitness nut who had installed a Nautilus exercise machine in an empty room of his dental suite so he could sweat and pump iron during the lunch hour. The result, according to the red book, was "a beautiful, glistening body, hard as iron, with not so much as one ounce of flabe, honest to God."

Les loved expensive cars:

> Today Lessie compared me to a car and I concidered it as a compliment! It is his brand new Jag XJ-6! He told me while we were cuppled you are exactly like my new Jag, creamy white, beautiful and powerful and I love to ride both of you. And I really gave him a good ride then for telling me that!

Les was a vegetarian, a Gucci shoe man, a Swarthmore graduate, a Jew who "takes deep pride in his Polish ethnic heritage," a dutiful and devoted husband to Heidi, a wonderful father to Rachel and Enoch, and "a world-class lay" who screwed Earline's socks off practically every afternoon after work in a hotel apartment he kept right across the street from his office. "Golden afternoons," she wrote. "Lanquid hours. Never did I dream a kike could be so exciting!"

I made her read it all to me and by the time she had finished I knew I wasn't going to kill her, never had intended to kill her, not really. I just wanted her to shame herself and, I suppose, shame me as well, but I succeeded only by half. When she finished the last page she flipped the book aside and said, "Satisfied? I just hope you're satisfied."

I stuck the gun inside the waistband of my trousers. "Stand up. And walk downstairs."

"Let me get a robe."

"No. Just walk."

There was only a small entrance foyer at the bottom of the staircase. When we got there, without saying a word, I threw open the front door and pushed her outside and slammed and locked the door behind her. Then I went into the living room, got my half-empty bottle of vodka, sat on the couch and waited. Had another drink. It was early December.

Somewhere, in the medical section of *Time* or in *Psychology Today*, somewhere I read that few people can take more than a couple of hard personal knocks one right after another without coming apart at the seams. Earlier that same day, before I came home and found the little red book, I had been fired after twenty-five years on the job.

I'm fifty and for half of those years I had worked for a Chicago newspaper I would rather not identify because it no longer exists. Its name exists, but it is a vulgar rag filled with sex and crime, edited by a gang of creeps, and owned by a right-wing egomaniac who bought it for a song from the childish, idiotic woman who inherited it.

Before the paper changed hands I was its chief investigative reporter. No great stylist, not an especially clever writer, although not all that bad, either. Most of all, a reporter who never wanted to be anything else, who ended up as one because I am the sort of person who has always liked to poke into things. Cops on the take, corrupt officials, unsolved crimes, scandals, swindles, those were my specialties. I won a Pulitzer for a series I did on conditions inside the state insane asylum.

I stayed on the job for a couple of months after the sale. Others who could afford to had cleaned out their desks and walked. But I needed the money. I had debts I won't go into. Who doesn't at my age? Earline's new red Corvette, and wasn't that just like her. Other things.

So I hung around while the new people took over, hired and fired, replacing a solid, reliable city room with an out-of-town bunch of fast-fingered goons who filled the news hole every day with murder, gossip, lotteries and tits-and-ass pictures. Praise the Lord for freedom of the press. I stayed on, hating it, hating myself, and drinking far too much.

I didn't eat lunch that day, didn't drink either, not at first. Instead I walked the windy streets of the city, wondering what the hell I was going to do. When I got back to the office I found a copy of the Late City edition on my desk. On the front page the lead story was one the goons had written under my byline. The huge headline read FORMER DEB AXED! The woman was fifty-eight and her crazy son had done it. I stormed into the editor's office yelling at the top of my voice and when I stormed out five minutes later, after twenty-five years on the job and never missing a deadline, I was on the bricks.

Earline rang the doorbell but I didn't answer it. I knew all the doors and windows were locked. We lived in a small town house about thirty minutes out of the city. Crime was no problem out there but Earline had a thing about it, so the house was wired with an alarm system so elaborate that your own shadow would set the thing off.

She pounded on the door and called me bad names. She lifted the mail slot and tried to reason with me, even begged and pleaded a little. I knew she had to be getting more than a little chilly because she was standing out there naked as a jaybird and the temperature was down around freezing. I went to the door, took a quarter from my pocket and pushed it through the mail slot. "Here. Call Les," I told her. "Call Les and tell him to come pick you up in his new Jaguar XJ-6." Then I sat down again and waited for her to make the next move.

A minute later the first brick came crashing through the picture window, a brick from the border I had placed around a flower bed.

Earline had been a truly beautiful young girl, married at nineteen, and her first husband, a discount appliance store owner, had commissioned an oil portrait of her, not a bad piece of work. It hung now, not properly in the bedroom or the study but over the living-room fireplace, and wasn't that just like her. When the second brick came crashing through the window, sending more glass flying through the room, I took careful aim with the .38 and blew the left eye out of her portrait.

It went on that way, with her throwing bricks and me shooting her painted head away, until somebody down the street called the cops.

I never should have shot up Earline's oil portrait. Les the dentist who loved Mozart found her a lawyer who called me and said he would like to meet with me "privately and confidentially, and totally off the record" before I retained counsel.

I agreed and we got together for lunch at The Town Club. If you were one of the city's up-and-coming heavy-hitters and neither a Jew nor a journalist, The Town Club was what you joined—indeed, if you could get in *there*—while you waited for a place to open up for you in The City Club, whose membership was older, richer, and more settled in their greeds and prejudices.

The lawyer was late but the twenty-minute wait was worth every minute of it because this was one more beautiful guy. He wore a custom-made shirt with a gold collar pin and gold cuff links, a blue suit by Brioni di Roma, a Turnbull & Asser tie, a half pound of solid-gold Rolex on his wrist, and the most beautiful pair of shoes I had ever seen. All he lacked was a page boy following him around with a big sign which said EXPENSIVE DIVORCE LAWYER.

Perrier and lime and the shrimp salad for him, thanks

George. I ordered hamburger steak with onion gravy, which is called trying to make a statement.

"I've asked you to meet informally with me because I would like to save both of us a lot of time and save you a lot of money," this young, well-dressed divorce lawyer said to me with a big Smile.

"Very thoughtful of you. You a friend of the family or what? You know . . . Heidi and the kids."

"Les and I are squash-racquets friends. Belong to the same club."

"Well, I can understand how you could get close, playing with each other regularly."

He didn't think that was very funny but he tried not to let his annoyance show. This was a busy guy on a tight schedule. No fooling around allowed. "Let me put it to you straight," he said. "I'm a busy man. Yes, I'm doing this as a favor to Les. Yes, I charge a very large fee for my services. And, yes, I'll end up losing money on this case. If you'll excuse my saying so, you're not a very fat cat."

"So what do you want?"

"Don't contest the divorce. I know she's fucking Les. But give her what she wants and walk away from it. Because if you don't, she's going to take you for everything you've got. Take my advice and save us all a lot of time and trouble."

"You know, it occurs to me that you're probably violating the state bar association's code of ethics, talking to me this way."

"Think it over. You haven't got that much money, number one. Number two, your old friends on the force covered for you about the unregistered revolver you blew your house away with. No charges filed. If we end up in court, I'll have to bring that out."

"You're saying you got my nuts in a stainless-steel vise?"

"She's got you, booby. You pushed her pretty hard and we have excellent pictures of the bruises. She bruises easily." He took a sip of his Perrier, nibbled at his shrimp.

I was weary and anxious to get it over with, which is the big mistake most divorced men vow never to make a second time. "What does she want?" I asked.

"Easy. Everything. That's an angry lady. And she'll get it, or most of it. Because you've got no real evidence to prove she's been banging Les."

"There's a diary."

He threw his arms back in mock amazement. "What diary? I have not seen or heard of any diary."

"A red diary."

"Excuse me, but is it in your possession?"

"Isn't that called destroying evidence?"

"Go search the house. Pick through the garbage if you like. I would bet you will not find any diary."

"Okay, I get the message."

"I mean you pushed her. You damaged the house." He pointed his finger at me. "And remember, the legal fee alone will bankrupt you if I have to take this to court. I guarantee it."

"Ten thousand to me. I shoved her out the door, that's all."

"Five. Five is all you get. Plus the old station wagon. She keeps the new Corvette and you maintain the payments. She gets your severance pay from the paper, plus the house. You get a settlement without alimony."

I motioned to the waiter. "Will you please take this hamburger steak away as it tastes like dog shit?"

"Take it or leave it," the young lawyer said. Had himself another forkful of shrimp.

"And bring me a big bowl of that bean soup that's your club specialty," I told the waiter. I looked at the lawyer.

"Seven. I'll take it. What else can I do?" I gave him a half-hearted salute. "You play hardball."

"Professionally, there's no other way."

The waiter brought the bean soup. "Oh, not for me," I told him. "For the other gentleman. Just put it in front of him."

"I don't want this soup." The waiter served him anyhow.

"You know, I like the way you dress," I told him. "Your clothes make a statement. Nice threads. And where'd you get the shoes? They may be the best damn looking pair of shoes I've ever seen."

"Florence, last summer."

I placed the sole of my right shoe on the top of his left one. "These old fuckers I'm wearing are Bostonians, I think." I started scuffing the top of his shoe. "Don't move your foot or I'll dump that bowl of bean soup in your lap." His body stiffened but he didn't move.

He sighed. "McFarland, you asshole."

"I get upset when people try to push me around. Divorce lawyers. Did you ever read much of Shakespeare? Somewhere I read that in one of his plays there's a line that says murder all the lawyers. I agree with that. Especially divorce lawyers, you bloodsuckers. So add the cost of these beautiful shoes to your bill." I had put my other shoe on top of his other one and now I was grinding away on both of them.

He laughed, a genuine laugh. "Jesus, you know what people in my line of work go through you wouldn't believe. Every husband wants to cold-cock us. Get even somehow. But ruin my shoes?" He laughed some more. "Go ahead, enjoy. I'll put it on the bill. And frankly it makes a hell of a funny story to tell my brethren."

I got out of my chair, stood beside him and put one hand on his shoulder. "You're right. Your brethren will get a kick out of the story. The shoes are funny," I said. "But the soup isn't." I tipped the bowl into his lap and walked away.

Okay, it was a mean and spiteful thing to have done but it did give me a certain sense of satisfaction. All I got besides that was my clothes, my personal papers and an old Ford wagon which needed new shocks and new brake linings, to say the least. A certified check for five thousand dollars was mailed to me after I signed the divorce agreement. Five, not seven. Take it and walk.

I was advised by a secretary in the slick lawyer's office to arrive at my house on a Tuesday at noon to pick up my things. I went by cab from the hotel apartment where I had been staying, don't ask how much a month if you don't want to see a grown man cry. My things had been packed in boxes and left on the front steps, and the key was in the old wagon. The picture window was boarded up with plywood. MouMou was locked inside a steel cage that had been placed on the front porch a few feet from my gear. There was a note taped to the cage that said: Dog Infirmery man, Please put this old dog to sleep as she is old and in constant pane. She is lieing on her favorite blankie, please bury her in it. Also my finance is illergic to dog hair. Thank you, Mrs. Earline McFarland.

I took the dog with me, put the cage in the back of the wagon, don't ask why.

Next I drove to a downtown bar and grill, had a hamburger and one drink too many and decided to wreak the most terrible vengeance I could imagine on Les the dentist who was allergic to dog hair. I made two stops, at a hardware store and a five-and-ten, then drove to the unattended parking garage next to his office where he kept his car. I found it down on the fourth level without difficulty, a white,

28

gleaming XJ-6, sure enough, with vanity license plates which said PAINLES. From a pay phone I called his office and told his secretary there had been a bad accident in the garage and what was the name of his automobile insurance company? That brought him running.

I stepped out of the shadows when he came barreling down the ramp, around the corner, and it brought him up short. "How you doing, Les?" I asked. I pulled the pistol from my jacket pocket and held it, barrel down, so he could get a good look at it. "I guess you know what this is."

"Yes sir."

"In case you missed it in the news, the Army's replacing all the old Colt forty-fives with Baretta nine millimeters."

"Mr. McFarland, there are a lot of things you don't know."

"I think I know all I need to know."

"It was Earline who instigated this problem, not me, sir. And I want to apologize. And I certainly hope you will accept my apology. You see, I'm a married man. Two kids. I'd sincerely love for you to meet them sometime."

"Take off your clothes."

"Sir?"

"I said take off your clothes. Strip, damn it. Down to your shorts. *Do it!*"

He obeyed me, removed his clothes piece by piece until he stood there in Gucci loafers, Polo socks and Jockey shorts, sweating and shivering.

I had bought a crowbar at the hardware store. I slid it across the concrete floor to him. "Pick it up and work over your car."

He looked down at the crowbar and I thought he was going to cry. "I'm terribly sorry but I just don't think I can do it, Mr. McFarland."

"You'll do it if you know what's good for you. Pick it up. Get moving."

He did it, sighing with each half-hearted swing, but swinging away, anxious to demonstrate his willingness to cooperate.

"Windows, windshield, hood, trunk, top, everything," I said. He loved that XJ-6. The car was spotless. He obviously spent twenty-five or thirty bucks a week having it worked over at some detail shop where they use old baby diapers and Q-Tips and clean everything right down to and including the hubcaps.

Soon he became angry. "To hell with this wreck," he said, working on the hood.

I was beginning to feel a little sick to my stomach. "Look, Earline's just an afternoon lay to you, but she was my wife. How would you feel if it had been me and your wife, what's her name, Heidi." I was apologizing to the son of a bitch.

"Fucking car!" he cried, still swinging away with the crowbar. "You want to see a trashed Jag just stick around, friend. I'm going to show you a trashed Jag."

"Stop," I said. "That's enough."

"You haven't seen anything yet. I'm going to show you a piece of junk."

"No, that's enough," I said. "Stop now and slide the crowbar back over to me." He hesitated for a moment, breathing hard, then did as he was told. I threw the crowbar down the ramp. "You shouldn't have done what you did, Les, and let this be a lesson to you. It's almost always a mistake to mess around with the help at the office. Now open your mouth."

He was afraid but he did it, not quite sure of what I was going to do next. I stepped forward and leveled the pistol at him, about two yards away from his face. It was a toy replica of a Baretta, an expensive water pistol I had bought at the five-and-ten, along with a bottle of mouthwash to fill it. I squirted him in his mouth. "Rinse, please," I said, turned and walked away. And vengeance was mine, I guess.

What a mess! Never take things for granted. From now on that's my motto because life can blow up in your face when you least expect it. A trite observation but it's still hard to take when it actually happens to you, believe me. One day you think you're more or less okay, hanging in there, and the next day old friends drinking after work will be saying, "Wonder what old Mac is up to these days. Anybody heard? He caught on anywhere yet?" Never dreaming that there you were, not a mile away, shooting a water pistol into a terrified dentist's face.

Is old Mac still in town? No. I hear he just got in that old car she let him have and took off. Hightailed it east until he saw a road sign that said Cape Cod. Never had been there so he turned off and ended up in some little town where there was an old lady killed and the town's police chief checked him out and told him to *non exite urbem sine me videndo*.

I walked over to a window, wiped away the frost and looked out at the backyard. There were four or five inches of snow on the ground now, maybe more. The wind was blowing and the long, thin limbs of the silver-leaf maples were swaying and creaking. Clam Pond was covered with a thickening skim of ice hard enough to hold a layer of snow. White and cold it was, with low gray skies, a bleak day. Only early afternoon and already dusk was setting in.

In the backyard, I noticed, somebody seemed to be making away with a load of my firewood.

THREE

I THOUGHT HE WAS A BUM. HE
was wearing thin gray cotton trousers tucked inside floppy,
unbuckled black overshoes and a gray tweed overcoat two
sizes too small for him which had seen far better days. A
black knit cap covered his head. No gloves. His hands were
raw and red. A bum, I thought, but a man who looked
quite fit for his age. I walked to within three or four yards
of him. His back was to me. "Good afternoon," I said.

"Oh, my God!" he yelled and threw the wood he was
carrying up in the air. Then, turning toward me, he stepped
on one of the logs, his foot shot forward, and he fell to the
ground.

"Are you hurt?"

"Who are you?" He was an old guy, a little dazed and a
little disoriented. He looked up at me tentatively, then
struggled to get back on his feet.

"Here, let me help you." I gave him a hand and pulled
him up. "I'm house-sitting here. And at the risk of seeming
a little pushy maybe you can tell me how you come off
helping yourself to my firewood."

He stared at me, speechless. "Try. Think hard," I said.
Treat bums like human beings, that's always been my idea,
flawed but human, not animals and not pets, people. This

bum's teeth were chattering. "Jesus, are you okay? Come on, let me get you inside the house."

"The wood. Please let me load my wood." He knelt and started gathering the wood he had dropped, and I thought that as a kid he might have served as an apprentice to Charles Chaplin. For every stick of wood he picked up he dropped another one. But he was fiercely determined and finally, with only half a load wrapped in his arms, he waded through the snow, down toward a faded old GMC pickup truck he had parked for some reason way down on the lawn, almost at the edge of the pond. He stumbled again on the way and fell to his knees, but got up and gathered himself together. By the time he reached his truck he had dropped half the small load he was carrying, one stick at a time as he struggled along, so that he had at best only three or four sticks left when he got there.

I trailed behind him, retrieving the wood he lost. When I reached the truck I found him down on his hands and knees, crawling around in the snow.

"Hey? Hey, you!"

"My glasses! I've lost my glasses. They slid off my nose. I'm blind without them."

A hopeless case. I got down with him and we crawled around together in the snow, patting, digging, sifting. No eyeglasses. "We'll never find them," I told him. "We're crawling around out here in the middle of a blizzard."

"I must. I simply must."

I hauled him to his feet. "Mister, we're both going to freeze to death out here. Come on." I put my arm around his shoulders and led him to the house, a wet, cold, bedraggled old man who kept saying "Oh, God" on the way.

I sat him on the couch in the living room, pulled off his wet overcoat and his overshoes, which he allowed me to do without protest, and threw more wood on the fire. I jerked a wool blanket off my bed, doubled it, and draped it over his shoulders, wondering if I should drive him to see a doctor.

"My name is Gerald Dickerson," he announced.

"My name is McFarland."

"No doubt you are wondering what I was doing in your yard, Mr. Farland," he said, looking at the whatnot in the corner which he thought was me.

"I'm over here. By the fire. Try to zero in on my voice, Mr. Dickerson. And yes I am."

"Well, I'm an old friend of the owner. I've cut down the dead trees on this property for countless years and used them for firewood. I had no idea anyone was staying here."

There was something about him, something immediately recognizable. There is something special about old New England men, something inherently gracious that is hard to explain. The accent? Those charming country manners? Their stiff, insistent yet gentle demeanor? Whatever, you could recognize them a mile away. There was one old man in North Walpole who smoked a pipe and when he had enough of it, he stuffed it in his jacket pocket, still lit. The smoke drifted out. That's what I'm talking about.

"Ah! Delicious!" Gerald Dickerson exclaimed, even before he had tasted the coffee I offered him. He reached out for the cup and saucer because he smelled the coffee, and he missed it by a foot to the left. "Just what one needs on a nippy day such as this, Mr. Farland."

"You know, you shouldn't be out in weather like this."

"You're right. Getting on, I'm afraid. Seventy-nine, almost eighty." The cup and saucer rattled in his hands and the coffee sloshed back and forth.

MouMou recognized class when she saw and smelled it and took an immediate liking to him, trotted over and nuzzled his leg with her head. "Well, hello there," he said. "Dog, is it?"

"More or less."

"Nice dog."

"Bitch. When I let her out she runs away and won't come back."

MouMou was so thrilled I thought she was going to pee on the hooked rug. Instead, quivering in ecstasy, she jumped into his lap and cuddled there, glowering at me with deep hostility.

"Not from around here, are you?" Mr. Dickerson said. With a shaking hand he attempted to bring the cup to his lips but spilled a splash of coffee on the floor in the process. "Oh, damn, damn. Sorry," he said as he carefully, slowly placed the coffee cup in the ashtray. "So you're *house-sitting*. Well, good for you." He made it seem as if I were doing voluntary missionary work in the outback of North Borneo. He made another go at the coffee and, using both hands, succeeded this time.

"Matt O'Neil was nice enough to let me bunk in. I'm just passing through, on my way to Boston."

"Jamie Hollings inherited this place. From a bachelor uncle, as I recall. Never lived here, never took any interest in it. A Californian. In fact, I don't know who owns the place now. It seems to me that I read in the alumni newsletter that Jamie is dead now. I taught him years and years ago at Saint Tim's. Little more than a boy myself at the time.

Saint Timothy's. The Eton of America. "You taught there?"

"For thirty-five years. Math and Latin." He waved his hand in abrupt dismissal of the subject. The past.

"But you live here now?"

"Since my retirement. I house-sit myself in winter. Have for years, same house, oh yes. But in the summer and early fall I live in the little guesthouse on the water's edge of Jane's property, on the other side of the hedge that divides her property from this place."

"You knew Mrs. Drexel? Mr. Dickerson, you *do* know what's happened?"

"Yes, yes. Quite awful. It's been on the radio news all morning long. I only hope and pray they catch the person who did it. Dear, dear Jane. I tell you, I'm still in a state of shock."

I walked over to the window beside the fireplace and looked out at the guest cottage which was located on the other side of the high privet hedge which divided the two properties. It was not very big, a little frame cottage only a few inches higher than the hedge that surrounded it. "I thought it was a gardener's shed."

"An old bathhouse, actually. Years ago a dock led from it out to the pond. But the pond's surface changed and Jane had the dock moved up fifty feet or so where the water's deeper and the bottom's sandy. Moved the dock but left the bathhouse. She swam off that dock every morning and every afternoon in the summer. For years."

"And you live there in the summers."

He nodded his head as he tried to drink more of his coffee, still using both hands to hold his cup. "Back, oh, in the early seventies, Jane decided to finance the college education of a few of North Walpole's less fortunate youngsters. Extremely bright children of good breeding, all of them, who simply didn't have the money for college. Jane approached me. Since my retirement here I've supplemented my income by tutoring summer boys who failed subjects in school the previous academic year. Usually Algebra One, God bless them. Frantic mothers, willing to pay anything. Jane decided to hold a summer school for the youngsters she'd selected, a general review session to get them off to a good start their freshman year in college. And the cottage was where we did it."

"And you ended up living there."

"I spent so much time there. I kept repairing this, re-placing that. The place was run-down, really hadn't been used for years. And Jane kept moving old things from the main house into the cottage, wicker chairs, old china, pots and pans, until at last she said to me that it looked as if she had acquired a permanent guest. Her idea, you see, not mine. Not that I protested all that much. It's a comfortable little spot."

"You two obviously were close friends."

"Yes, yes. Good buddies. I shall miss her terribly."

I don't know why I didn't just drop it. I wasn't all that interested. Just plain bored. You can only talk so much to a surly old bitch-dog who hates your guts. "Did you see her during this visit?"

"Alas, I did not."

"Have you talked to Chief Simmons yet? I'm sure he's going to want to have a chat with you."

He jumped up, sending MouMou tumbling to the floor, and placed his hand over his mouth. I thought he was going to throw up. The dog barked at him anxiously.

"Please sit down," I said. "Please. You know, I've seen a few other people as shook up as you are right now. But not all that many. Exactly what is your problem? Mr. Dickerson, were you at Mrs. Drexel's house last night?"

He dropped his coffee cup. Somehow I had known he would. It fell from his hands and broke on the floor. No loss, an old piece of dime-store junk. Plenty more where that came from, bought by summer tenants and left behind.

"You're afraid of something. You're scared out of your wits."

He wiped his eyes. "Quite right. Most perceptive."

"It doesn't exactly take a genius to see it, you know. I mean, you are a mess."

"I am quite terrified, Mr. Farland."

"It's *Mc*Farland. My friends call me Mac."

"I am terrified, Mac."

"Of what? Do you know something about Mrs. Drexel's death?"

"Mac? May I borrow your hog?"

"My what? My hog? I don't have a hog, Mr. Dickerson."

"Of course, I mean your *dog*. Your dog."

"No problem. Christ, you can have her."

He shook his head in despair. His was a handsome old face. He had a strong chin, a Tyrone Power chin, with dimples, and a head of thick white hair which he hadn't cut in months. "I wasn't being truthful when I said I hadn't been in communication with Jane. She called me at home yesterday afternoon, which gave me quite a start because I hadn't even known she was in town. Don't get out much in weather such as this. She invited me to come to lunch with her today, this very day."

"And what's wrong with that? But you ought to tell Chief Simmons about it. He needs every bit of information possible at this point in his investigation."

"I'm a poor man, Mac. Just my Social Security and a small pension from Saint Tim's."

"Believe me, without going into detail, I know what you mean."

"Jane gave me money."

"Of course she did."

"From time to time. Over the years. Never anything big. Initially she called it bonuses for my tutoring. Later, presents. The amounts varied. Five hundred here, three hundred there. Whatever she thought appropriate. A thousand dollars once for Christmas. It helped out."

"I'm sure it must have. But why are you telling me this?"

"I'm getting to that. It wasn't easy for me to take the money, Mac. You didn't know her. There were two sides to Jane. One was loving and giving, warm and outgoing, and the other was spiteful, haughty and cold. Almost like a split personality. Jane was in her late seventies, you must remember. Like me. And she was in the process of becoming senile, I'm afraid. She suffered from memory lapses, more and more as her mind began to deteriorate over the past year or so. At least, I think she did. One could never be sure about Jane."

"You mean she'd forget she hadn't given you anything lately?"

"No. Jane didn't forget to give me money. She began to forget where she'd hidden it. Or maybe she was just playing games with me, as usual. I truly don't know. I never asked her for money. And when she gave me any I always wrote a proper thank-you note. In the summer when I was in my cottage and she was in the big house I would get up early and pick a small basket of the wild raspberries that grow on the shore of the pond and leave them, together with a note of thanks, on the dock. That way she would find them when she came down for her morning swim. Or sometimes I would rinse and sugar the raspberries and bring them to her with a pot of coffee, and we would swim together and eat and drink."

I thought of Earline. I thought of a younger Jane Drexel swimming in Clam Pond on a summer morning, a smile on her face. I thought of her sitting on her dock, eating sugared berries and drinking hot coffee. And I thought of Earline, whose usual topic of conversation at dinner was the size of the hunks of plaque she had scraped off her patients' teeth that day. "I swear to God, as big as these kernels of corn we're eating."

"Jane loved her tricks and surprises, liked to make me sweat a little," Gerald Dickerson said. "I'd find an envelope on the seat of my truck with five one-hundred-dollar bills inside it. Or, once she took a bank-deposit slip of mine which she got at my cottage and put a thousand dollars in my checking account. I didn't know the money was there, and she didn't say a word about it. I didn't know until the monthly statement arrived."

"She wasn't senile. She just liked to play games with you."

"I suppose. But she liked to give me the impression that she was absentminded. For example, I very much enjoy reading Latin poetry in bed at night. Early last summer I was reading Ovid. *The Art of Love*. Really masterful elegiacs. And there, tucked in the pages, were three hundred-dollar bills. I asked her and she said, 'You fool, I kept using the word *erotic* constantly for days as a clue.' "

"I can see where this could be a problem. Hard clues."

"Jane could be thoughtful and spiteful at the same time. Yesterday afternoon on the phone she said I was getting on in age, as if she weren't as well, and that she had decided I needed a sizable sum of money to make me more comfortable and secure over the winter. So, she told me, she was going to give me ten thousand dollars."

I whistled sincerely.

"But she said, too bad for me, the money was all in frozen assets. I said I simply didn't understand. Frozen assets. She said it was a mystery and she was going to let me suffer a bit while I tried to figure it out. The other, dark side of Jane, you see."

"Maybe she intended to give you another clue today at lunch."

"Perhaps. Who knows? I *do* know she would have drawn it out. Teased me until I was at the boiling point. It was her way."

"And you think she left the money somewhere in that cottage? Right?"

"The thought struck me while I was listening to a report of her death on the radio this morning. WCIB. I like their weatherman, Harvey Leonard. He's a trained meteorologist, you know. And usually quite dependable. Misses now and then. But they all do."

I waited for him to get to the point. Most people his age need a little time to do that.

"I was shocked by the report of her death, of course. But I could not help but think back on our last conversation. Jane, you see, was a mystery-book fan. Loved Agatha Christie. Mystery novels with clues. Mac, I think she gave me a clue in our phone conversation."

"Frozen assets?"

"She can't have meant she hid it in the yard somewhere, in the snow. At least I don't think so. Frozen assets. I think she was hinting that she had put the money in my refrigerator. Or perhaps in hers, in the main house. But, of course, it's under guard."

We sat there. He stroked MouMou's back. I lit a cigarette. I would have put another log on the fire but the fire didn't need another log. We sat there and thought about ten thousand dollars.

"That's why you were out in the yard, pretending to load wood. You were trying to work up the courage to go down to the cottage and see if the money's there."

"I'm not a brave man. I'll admit it. I'm terrified to go near the cottage because I know it's probably being watched. But do you know what that money would mean to me? I could get all my bills paid up. Buy a new winter suit for church. I haven't had a new suit of clothes in fifteen years."

"And that truck looks like it's about time to have some work done on it."

"Brake linings, tires, a major tune-up, just about everything short of a new engine."

"And something for yourself. A man needs to buy himself a little something every now and then."

"A digital watch. I want a digital watch. There's one at

the Alden variety store I've had my eye on. Forty dollars. That and a small collection of liqueurs. I love a sweet liqueur at night before bed. Kahlúa. Drambuie."

"That doesn't seem out of line at all to me, Mr. Dickerson. I mean, that's not asking for the moon or anything in my book."

"There are the toilers in the South African mines. There are sweatshop laborers. There are migrant farm workers. And there right with them there are private secondary schoolteachers. Such as I was."

"I know there's not much money in it."

"Not much even today, nothing when I did it. You live on nothing and you end up with nothing."

"I'm a newspaperman. It comes to about the same thing."

"They dedicate annuals to us. I had three different Saint Tim yearbooks dedicated to me."

"They give us prizes. You should see all the prizes I got, all framed and packed away."

"If there is such a thing as reincarnation I want to come back either as a lapdog or a full professor at MIT. Make a good salary teaching young people of superior intelligence a couple of classes a week. Serve on two or three company boards. Travel all over to seminars and the like. Haul in a bundle. Better than being a lapdog."

I took his cup, poured him more coffee, then carefully placed the cup back in his hands.

"My students all were dressed in Brooks Brothers or J. Press, head to toe. Half of them were heirs to trust funds. Set for life before they took the first step down the road. I used to go and search their rooms when the school year ended, looking for jackets and sweaters they had discarded. Perfectly good clothing, some of it hardly worn."

"Mr. Dickerson, I think I know what it is you want from me. And the answer is no."

"You happened to mention the fact that your dog has a propensity for running away when you let her out. I thought if we let her out it would give us a reason for taking a walk down there. I have my key, would have gone in myself. But now I can't see."

"There was a murder committed on that property last night."

"We won't go inside. We'll just go around to the kitchen window which looks out on the pond. We can see the refrigerator from there. I have a strong flashlight in my truck."

"And what if the money's there? If Noah Simmons is half the cop I think he is, he's already got a police lock on the door. *I* would. As a general precaution."

"I'll worry about that when the time comes. I'm desperate to have a look and we've only a precious few minutes of light left. You see, I'm almost certain I cleaned out the refrigerator when I moved out in September, unplugged it and left the door open, the way I always have done. If the door *is* open we can look into the refrigerator, through the window, and see if the money's there."

"And if the door is closed it means she could have put the money there and closed it."

"I must have a look. And I'm asking your help, even though we are perfect strangers."

"That's right. I don't even know you and we are talking about murder here, Mr. Dickerson."

"I have no one else to turn to. I'm pleading for your help."

"I appreciate your problem but I've got troubles of my own."

"Is it a cut you want? I'll give you twenty-five percent."

"No, damn it. No!"

And, of course, I went with him. Impulse. It is a powerful factor in the lives of all of us. Young sailors get tattoos of hearts and dragons in Oriental ports. Big winners in Vegas marry perfect strangers in drive-in chapels. Listen, you guys, if we quit talking about it and leave right now we can be in Florida by daylight. I quit, take this job and shove it. I'll buy it. What the hell, I'll go up there and take that point for you, Lieutenant.

"Okay," I said. "But we will not touch that cottage. We'll go down and take a look, look through the kitchen window. But that's it."

"I give you my word, Mac. And God bless you."

He got MouMou's pullover sweater on her while she sat on his lap and trembled with pleasure. Then he and I bundled up and set out with him carrying the dog in his arms, preceding me, which was a big mistake because he stumbled and fell face-forward off the front steps, into the snow. MouMou went flying. That was the first thing that happened.

I got him up and had him sit on the steps. "Missed that last one I'm afraid. Sorry, Mac," he said, brushing the snow off his face. The snow was falling harder than ever and visibility was extremely limited. "A real Cape Cod blow, that's what it's turned into," he said.

"Don't move. Sit there. I'll be right back." I went into the kitchen and got a length of clothesline I'd noticed there. I tied one end around my waist and the other around his, two bowlines, the only knot I knew: *Rabbit comes out of his hole, runs around the trunk of the tree and goes back in.* I recited the old memory aid aloud, can't you just see me, as I tied the knots, he gathered up MouMou, who had been pawing around him, very concerned about his welfare, and we set out, again. "Let's check out the front first, see how many cops we're dealing with," I said, giving the line a pull.

In a snow like that—at some point, at some time of fading light—dimensions become obscure as details are covered

44

and rounded and as ordinary sights—trees, bushes, posts— assume new, strange shapes. Everything looks different, altered, a strange yet familiar land.

We made our way carefully through the yard, going from tree to tree, and crouched behind the thick line of snow-choked evergreen hedge which grew along the front of the property, the divider between the Hollings place and Clam Pond Drive.

There was, thanks to the modern miracle of radio and television news, a traffic jam on the road. Jane Drexel's death was big, big news in North Walpole and in all surrounding communities and, it seemed, everybody wanted to brave the weather and come out and take a firsthand look at the place where it had happened. Both lanes of Clam Pond Drive, we could see through the hedge, were filled with slowly moving cars. A police squad car, red and blue top lights rotating, blocked the entrance to the Drexel driveway and a policeman with a portable, hand-held loud-speaker stood beside it, repeating traffic instructions. "Keep moving, let's keep moving, folks. Nothing here to see. No stopping please."

Only one guy on duty, so far as I could tell. I gave Mr. Dickerson a tug on the line and we headed back toward his cottage, following a second line of hedge which ran between the Hollings place and Jane Drexel's property, the hedge MouMou had run through when I found the body. On the way we drifted apart, a gap of only a few feet but enough for him to get in trouble. He walked straight into a tree. Bloodied his nose and said, "Oh, damn, damn, damn! What a bloody nuisance! But I have a handkerchief. No real harm done. Let's keep going." Gerald Dickerson really wanted to take a look at that refrigerator.

So on we went, at times up to our knees in snow, and with almost zero visibility now. Mr. Dickerson stumbled and fell, but got up quickly, brushed himself off, somehow managing to keep MouMou within the fold of one arm, and walked right into the rear of his pickup truck. I hadn't seen it either.

I got him up, dusted him off, and shortened the length of the line so that now only a foot or two separated us. He opened the door of his truck and got a flashlight from the glove compartment. He had driven the truck within a few feet of the pond's edge, close to the hedge. The summer cottage was just on the other side.

There was an opening. We went through, and we had just reached the cottage when, on the pond, a bright light suddenly appeared, sweeping in a low arc across the iced surface. A searchlight? "I don't know about this," I said. "That looks like a police boat to me."

But the old man was not to be denied. He let MouMou fall from his arms and she disappeared into the snow. "Here, dog, here, here," he called out in a loud voice as he mushed resolutely around the corner of the cottage. "Mac! I do believe she's somewhere in the back here. Let's have a look."

MouMou, meanwhile, in love and blind to the old man's exploitation of her, was not trying to get away. She was trying to get to him, resurfacing briefly again and again as she plowed through the snow. Romantic old bitch.

"MouMou? MouMou?" Mr. Dickerson called urgently. She reached his feet. "*Get away!* Do get away, you wicked dog."

"For God's sake," I said. "Pick her up before she drowns."

"Now I can't see her. MouMou? MouMou?"

I bent down and caught the dog on the fly the next time she surfaced. We were at the back of the cottage, on the water side. MouMou was struggling in my arms, trying to get to Mr. Dickerson.

"I can't see anything, Mac," he whispered to me. "Except there seems to be a light on in the kitchen for some reason. What can you see? Can you see the refrigerator? Is it open? Is the money there?"

"Mr. Dickerson, you're not looking through the kitchen window. There's no light on in the kitchen. You're looking out at the pond. The light you see is a searchlight on a police boat. And it's time we got out of here."

It was at that moment that the Creature from the Black Lagoon surfaced, rose out of the waters of Clam Pond, cracking through the brittle ice and sending it flying in all directions. Huge, shining black, wreathed in a blinding light, it came lumbering out of the water and through the frozen layers of marsh grass, toward us. *"Ave, doctor veneratus!"* it said to Mr. Dickerson.

It was North Walpole's police chief, Noah Simmons, dressed in a black scuba-diving outfit with a small light mounted on his head. He pulled off the light and his face mask. "It's Noah," he said.

"Oh, Noah! *Salve. Salve in hac die lachrymosa.*"

"I know. We'll all miss her." The creature put one of his huge black rubber arms around the old man.

"The dog ran away. In case you're wondering what we're doing out here," I said.

"Oh. Yes," Mr. Dickerson said. "And we must find her. Poor dog. Here, doggy, here."

"Here you go." MouMou wiggled out of my arms to get into his.

"Why, here she is, safe and sound. You naughty dog. We've been looking all over for you."

"Mr. Dickerson lost his glasses in the snow while we were tracking down MouMou," I said to Noah. "What were you looking for in the pond? Anything to do with the Drexel case?"

47

"No. Rocko Murphy. Fisherman. He clams here in the pond between trips out to the banks. His wife's reported him missing, which isn't unusual because Rocko's a hell-raiser. Except the Coast Guard found his clamming boat adrift earlier this afternoon. So I was taking a look, even though I'm sure he'll turn up in a bar somewhere. I saw your light when I surfaced so I came over to see who you were."

Mr. Dickerson gave him a pat on his back. "Noah knows this pond like the back of his hand. All the waters around here, for that matter. He should have been a marine biologist. I've always said so."

"*Doctor veneratus*, I *am* a marine biologist. Remember? You attended my graduation, you and Mrs. Drexel."

"Of course. Of course you are. How nice for you. He loves these waters, Noah does. Gave the commencement address in Latin. Indeed. I recall it now. My best Latin student ever, by far."

"Has it occurred to anybody else that we're standing out here freezing to death?" I said.

"Yes. Let's get you home now, Doctor D.," Noah said. And the old man in his old, thin clothes was, indeed, in sad shape. We all needed to get inside. People like to say they like a spot of cold weather and what they really like is refuge from it, big fires, drink which thaws the bones, warm rooms and cozy beds.

But, cold as he was, Gerald Dickerson still had that ten thousand dollars on his mind. "As long as we're here, there's a paring knife—" he said. "A small paring knife. I think I must have left it behind when I packed and left in September. I think I'll just go inside and take a look for it. Won't take a moment. I've got my key. You two just stay where you are." He turned his flashlight back on and headed for the front door of the cottage.

"It's padlocked," Noah said. "And I don't have a key. I threw a police lock on it this morning. And you're going to catch pneumonia if you don't get home and into a hot tub."

"Mr. Dickerson came over for some firewood and his truck got stuck," I said. Noah stared at me and I decided on the spot to keep my mouth shut and let them work it out, teacher and student. After all, I was a stranger to the Cape myself.

"If there is any way you could get the key to the padlock I would be most appreciative of it, Noah." Almost a plea.

"I'll get your truck pulled out and over to you tomorrow," Noah Simmons said. "Now come on, I'll get a squad car to take you home." He reached down, pulled off his flippers, then stood, this huge man, scooping a startled Gerald Dickerson up in his arms.

"Noah, I am perfectly capable of making my own way," the old man cried. "And I would give anything to get that knife."

"We'll worry about your knife later. Right now I'm getting you to bed," Noah said, carrying him away. He stopped, turned and looked at me. "I'll be having breakfast tomorrow morning at Bob's. Around seven. If you're interested."

"I'll be there."

He walked away with the old man in his arms. Whispering to him. "You shouldn't be out in weather like this."

FOUR

I FOUND IT HARD TO SLEEP
that night. I ate a frozen Mexican dinner I heated up in
the toaster oven, drank beer, and tossed and turned as
usual; there finally comes a time when you can't sleep that
you curse it and challenge it, which was the state I was in.

Sometime early in the morning the floor furnace cut off
for some reason, the fire died down, the living room got
cold and I didn't have the pioneer spirit to get up and try
to deal with it. So I lay there, covered with two thick wool
blankets, and waited out the hours, thought about Earline.
Couldn't help myself. I reflected on the fact that I was
damn near broke and unemployed. No plans. A burnt-out
case. Cheerful things like that which you'd think would lull
a guy right off to sleep.

My little G.E. electric alarm clock which sat on the floor
was set for six. When it buzzed I stuck one foot from under
the cover and MouMou, who had been lying patiently on
the sheepskin nightnight I'd bought her, waiting for the
opportunity, bit me on my big toe and scurried under the
couch. The beginning of another perfect day with a loving
dog at one's side.

I dressed quickly, then got down on my knees in front
of the couch and, looking at two weak, pink eyes glaring
back at me, said, "Okay. You stay there. Starve. Die. Freeze

to death. It's well below freezing in this room, you know. Well below freezing. And I am going to Bob's Sandwich Shop where it's nice and toasty warm. I'm going to have myself a nice, hot breakfast while you lie there and shiver . . . unless you want to come with me. Want to come?" A bleak look, no response. To hell with her.

The old car started without delay, wonder of wonders, and somehow I made it, sliding and twisting out of the frozen driveway, onto the road. The town had done a good job plowing and sanding overnight and the main road was clear. It was a cloudless blue-sky day, still very cold, but yesterday's snowstorm had passed out to sea during the night, leaving behind a little Cape Cod town which, well, really did look like an idyllic Kodachrome scene on a picture postcard.

The town's character changed in winter. I know that because summer was the favorite topic of conversation with the people I talked to at the Binnacle and the Buckaneer. Last summer, like a young love.

During summer, really only July and August, North Walpole's population approaches thirty thousand and that is when you make it if you're a merchant. Make it or else. Main Street is filled with expensive automobiles from New York and Boston and New Jersey, and the sidewalks are clogged with tourists with money in their pockets. All the restaurants are open with long waiting lines outside and with fresh-faced college kids working as waitresses and busboys. The antique shops have handmade quilts on display. Pilgrim Harbor is filled with yachts and motor cruisers. Affluent teenagers wearing T-shirts emblazoned with charging polo ponies enact their mating rituals on the beaches and at lighted poolsides, drinking imported beer, while their parents, dressed in bright, vivid summer clothes, thrill the stores with their purchases, drink vodka on the porches and patios and speak in awe and smug self-satisfaction about the rising real estate prices. There is a band concert in the park every Friday night at eight and people come from miles around, bringing blankets and folding chairs, jugs of coffee and iced daiquiris. The band plays marches and show tunes and always ends with a waltz so booze-sodden couples may stagger around humming "Good Night, Sweetheart." Nice summer evenings, those. The kids race their sloops in the harbor and boogy-board behind Boston whalers in the salt ponds and fish for flounder off the bridges. At Simmons' Fish Market fresh lobster and swordfish arrive every day, brought in by the Cape fishermen in their rusty boats. Get a five-dollar license at city hall and you can dig up all the littleneck clams and mussels you'd ever want to eat right on the public beaches, a bucket of each a day. A beautiful place, a retreat, a refuge, if you made enough money during the winter in Boston or New York to afford it in the summer.

In the winter the town closes down and boards up, and the population drops to less than five thousand. SEE YOU NEXT SUMMER! proclaim the signs in the windows of the emptied leather shops and art galleries, whose owners have shifted operations to Santa Fe and Delray Beach. Main Street becomes almost deserted and there are plenty of parking spaces any time of day. The movie theater is open, one show only, on Monday, Wednesday and Friday nights. It's hard to find an open bar or a reasonably good place to eat.

Winter is when the natives of North Walpole reclaim their town or try to. More and more retired people are wintering over. And there are the winter dropouts, a special group of people of varying age groups who work hard during the summers, hoard the money they make, then house-sit, drink beer and watch television on huge color cable screens as caretakers in absent millionaires' homes. A few teach school, but most do nothing during these dreary months.

The winter-morning hangout in North Walpole was Bob's Sandwich Shop on Main Street, next door to the movie theater. It was where everybody came to buy the morning papers, to eat that morning's fresh doughnuts and to drink coffee brewed only minutes ago, a place to meet and talk and gossip, where everybody knew everybody else. That was Bob's. Almost every small town has one. Is there any place more inviting?

I got there shortly before seven that Wednesday morning and found a parking place right in front. The windows were steamy and the place was filled. The regulars all were there, joking and greeting one another, and there was the smell and sound of hot, brown toast popping, eggs frying on the grill, and bacon sizzling. I took the last available counter seat and ordered coffee. No appetite for some reason. Noah Simmons was not there. I was no regular but I sensed that every eye in the place was on me: His name escapes me, but he's the one who found her, isn't he? Been in town a couple of weeks. Comes in here sometimes.

I hadn't been there five minutes when a young uniformed policeman came in, looked around and walked over to me. "You're McFarland, right? I was out at Mrs. Drexel's yesterday."

"I'm supposed to meet the chief for breakfast."

"He says to tell you he can't make it. He'll see you later. Had to go to Barnstable. Also, there was a telephone call for you over at headquarters. Somebody from the Boston *Globe*." He pulled out his notebook, the way cops do it, and read from it. "David Farkas. Ring a bell?" He gave me a phone number. I thanked him and immediately went to the pay phone in the back of the café, next to the rest rooms. When David Farkas came on the line his first words to me were, "Mac, is that you?" He was an old friend, a guy I had come to know when we both were assigned to cover the southern civil rights troubles. "I've been trying like hell to get in touch with you," he said.

"How did you learn I'm here?"

"The police chief mentioned your name. I heard you left that rag which formerly was a newspaper and I don't blame you. But Cape Cod in January?"

"I'm here trying to find myself, the real me." Not funny. I was embarrassed, didn't know what else to say.

"Well, how would the real you like to do me a big favor? I'm regional editor here now. Can you string for me for a couple of weeks?"

"The Drexel thing?"

"You got it. She was big Boston money, you know, so there's a lot of interest in the story here. We got a stringer on the Cape who's okay but not worth much on something like this. Nice old lady. I sent one of our best young general-assignment guys down yesterday but can you believe he's called in sick. Flu bug's going around. Half my staff is down with it. Can you help me out?"

I let it hang for a second, but only for a second. Be still my heart. "Sure, I'll string for you, do you a favor, Dave."

"Terrific. Just terriffic! Look, will five hundred a week cut it? I'm talking full-time coverage. I know you're worth far more but my budget's killing me right now."

"Sure. Five's fine."

"Terrific! Send me a picture, any snapshot will do, and a Social Security number and I'll get a press card made up for you. Need a car, get a rental. I'll wire you, what?, four hundred for initial expenses. And I'll mail you some expense-account forms. File your copy on the phone, this number. And, Mac, I'd like a piece for tomorrow. I'm told

54

the will will be filed in probate today. Seven hundred, seven-fifty words? Six o'clock deadline. It's a hell of a good story. Lots of money involved and a good, juicy society murder. So just let her rip in the classic McFarland manner I admire so much."

"You got it, Dave. No sweat."

"I can't give you a byline under this arrangement so it'll have to be Special to the *Globe*, okay? But as far as I'm concerned you're a world-class reporter and it's an honor to have you working for us. When this story is over let's talk. I really want you on the paper if you're interested. Got to go now, phone's going crazy."

That is what David Farkas, the regional editor of the Boston *Globe*, said to me that morning. Whole thing took only a couple of minutes.

I had some breakfast. I drank orange juice, cold milk, and black coffee, ate eggs, bacon, sausage—best breakfast I ever had in my life. I even had them poach two eggs for MouMou. "Damn right," I said to myself as I drove home with the eggs in a bag. "World class."

How long had it taken me to land on my feet? Less than two months, sooner if I had pushed it and asked around. Newspaper editors all over the country knew me by name and reputation, the same way Dave Farkas did. World class. His description.

I made it almost back to the house before I pulled off the road beside that part of Clam Pond that was used as a municipal swimming beach in the summer. Deserted now, with the lifeguard shack shuttered and locked. I stopped the car and rested my head on the steering wheel. Don't cry often.

They say traveling salesmen get by on a smile and a shoeshine. Well, news reporters make it on an ego and a byline. The knowledge that everybody in town is reading and talking about that big exclusive you came up with. The compliments. One hell of a story, Mac, my man. The intense satisfaction gained from being an independent journalist backed by a trusting and protective institution. Apple of the *Times*. Cannon of the *Post*. When you get that yanked away from you without warning you become an overnight nobody. And, besides, who doesn't feel a little insecure in this day and age?

Take your three-martini society surgeon who returns to the classy dinner party after leaving to perform an emergency operation and begins to wonder, over brandy, if he removed that little sponge before the patient was sewn up. Or your up-and-coming contractor whose first high rise starts to sink just a little on one side when they're topping off the twenty-fifth floor. Or the new guy who stands at the very tippy top of the killer no-net high-wire balancing act and starts getting leg cramps. Insecurity-wise we reporters rank right up with the very best of them.

But now I had credentials once again. McFarland of the *Globe*. It's like when the doctor says your case of the clap is all cured.

I blew my nose on a tissue, took a few deep breaths and raised my head. It scared the hell out of me, looking at me that way. A fat, arrogant seagull had planted itself on the warm hood of my car, inches away from the windshield, and was peering, curious he was, at the crying man.

"Quit glaring at me, you son of a bitch. Get out of here," I yelled. I haven't lost a step, I told myself. I've still got it, I could still catch the ball down the middle lane and take the jolt from the linebacker. I knew I had myself one hell of a story, an attention grabber which, if I handled it the right way, could put me back on my feet. It was a break, a little good luck for a change, and I was determined to take full advantage of it. "Get," I yelled. And the bird flew away.

I drove home, fed the eggs to MouMou and did my exercises for the first time since the last night with Earline. Sit-ups, knee-bends, touch-toes, push-ups, fifty of each. That's all I do, never increasing the numbers. Never jog, never run in place. That way leads to death. Then I took a shower—the electric hot-water heater worked, thank God— put on my best suit, armed myself with a notebook and a black Pilot Razor Point pen, and set out. A high school sophomore dressed out for his first varsity game, running out on a football field in September, that was how I felt. Send me in, Coach, I don't smoke. I haven't had a cigarette since the season started.

I drove to Barnstable, about an hour away. The clerk of the probate court there was so small he could have bought his clothes in any boys' department. "Hello there, big guy, what can I do you for?" he asked me.

"I'm McFarland of the *Globe*." First time I'd ever said it aloud. I liked the sound of it.

"McFarland of the *Globe*?" The little clerk held out his hand. "I'm Jimmy Olsen. Of the *Daily Planet*. You know— Superman? Except I can't help it because that's my real name." He had a bright open face and a big friendly smile.

"I'd like to take a look at the Drexel will. I understand it was filed today."

"And right you are, friend. All that money. Everybody has been wondering what'll happen to all that money." He studied my face. "Name sounds familiar. Are you on television? Do I see you on the booby-tubey?"

Courthouse people come in all shapes and sizes. Sour, fat ladies in girdles who can't hear you or see you waiting until it suits them. Grouchy old men who must assert their limited authority, tell you the rules. Young Mrs. Juggs with the beehive whom all the sheriff's deputies want to screw. Best way to deal with the worst of them is kick them in the teeth straight off, to get their attention. But not Jimmy Olsen, who was bright and chipper, a Chatty Chester and everybody's friend.

"No, you didn't see me on the booby-tubey, Jimmy. I'm the guy who found her. You read my name in the papers and it stuck with you."

"Of course you are. And it must have been horrible for you. Tell me about it. Did you barf? They always do when they find the bodies in crime novels."

"I can't begin to tell you. Can I see the will?"

"Why, of course. You know, most people don't realize it but the very reason for probate is to allow the general public the chance to take a look at any will. In case of a challenge, you know. To prove its validity. I mean, you don't have to be a reporter or anything like that." He handed me a copy of the Drexel will. "Enjoy. You're the first. But I'll guarantee you every living soul in North Walpole will want to take a look at this little beauty."

I read it.

"Not that it tells you much," Jimmy Olsen said. "What do you think? Not much there, is there? I live up in North Walpole, you know. Born there."

"What do you think?"

"I think this is going to set that town on its ear is what I think."

I took a few notes and handed the will back to him. "Thanks, Jimmy."

"No sweat. You know, we don't get excitement like this around here very often."

"I should think not."

"Mostly we get off watching the Celts and the Pats and the Red Sox. You a sports fan? I'm a nut, especially baseball. You a baseball nut by any chance?"

"Not so much now. I used to be."

"You ever play? You look like you could be a pitcher to me."

"A long time ago. High school and college and one season of Class A. Clinton, Iowa. San Francisco farm club."

"I can usually tell. You're looking at the coach of the North Walpole Pilgrims. Little League."

I was learning never to make snap judgments about Cape Codders because often they are more—or less—than they appear to be. The man in the expensive suit in the pew in front of you at church turns out to be the town's garbage collector. The guy who reads the water meter plays the cello in the string quartet. Jimmy Olsen was North Walpole's Little League coach and I would have bet that his first baseman was a head taller than he.

"You going to be around?" he asked. "I could sure use a pitching coach."

"I'll have to let you know about that, Jimmy. My plans are very uncertain at the moment."

"I love the game. Always did, since I was a kid. Shortstop on my high school team. Far as I got. Good field, no hit, like they say. Longest was a double and I still remember it. I would have given an arm and a leg for your Class A season."

"How'd your kids do last year?"

"Don't ask or I'll cry. But wait till this summer." He leaned over the counter. "I have a secret weapon. You are going to love this." He walked back to his desk and got a framed photograph of a really big woman and four of the fattest children I had ever seen, three boys and a teenage girl, and, except for their obesity, good-looking youngsters all of them.

"Look at this boy here, on this end," Jimmy Olsen said to me. "Already weighs a hundred and seventy. He couldn't play last year because he was just underage. But this year?

He can throw a baseball like Bob Feller. The problem is he's wild."

"They're . . . all yours?"

"Treat them like Patton, that's my motto. And that's my wife, Delores."

"Healthy-looking woman."

"Big as a whale. And strong as a horse. Kids get it from her." He leaned over the counter and whispered. "I'll tell you a little secret. She's really too big for me to handle so when I get, well, ready for it, in the mood, you know, I just make her strip down and get in the bathtub. Just lay her down in the tub. Works like a charm. Only way I can handle all that volume, little guy like me. In the tub I fit right in there."

"You do it in the bathtub."

"Try it sometime you find yourself with a fat lady. Delores is almost as big as Noah. No doubt you've met Noah."

I could see the strong resemblance in her freckled face. "The police chief."

"On the money. She was Delores Simmons. My high school sweetheart. Grade school, too, for that matter."

"Jimmy, the only thing is, I don't know if I'll still be around this spring. But if I am, sure, I'll give you a hand. Maybe we could take your boy out and work with him a little."

"Mac, I'd love that. You know, it's such a thrill watching the kids pick up the basic techniques of the game, getting better as the season goes on. Fun to see them to begin to appreciate the dimensions of the game and how complex and difficult it is to play well. I may not produce kids who go on to the pros, but I do produce great baseball fans. But with this boy? Arm like an ape."

"I can't promise you a curve. Or a slider. Nothing like that, not at his age. But maybe we can work a little on control and follow through, teach him how to use his body."

"Which he has plenty of. That's what he needs. And I would appreciate it, Mac. It'll be an honor to have him coached by a former pro."

"Just barely one, Jimmy."

He walked me to the door. "The murder's the talk of the town, to say the least. And a lot of people are wondering about you, living next door and all."

"Only natural."

"I'll put out the word you're okay. Bascombe Midgeley's the person you want to talk to next, I would think."

"The lawyer back in North Walpole. His name's on the will."

"One hundred Main Street. Second floor. Bascombe will try to big-deal you, Mac. He does that with people from out of town. Can't help it. It's his way. But he's bright and straight enough. Small-town Cape Cod boy. He just doesn't like to admit it. I've known him all my life."

"Thank you for your advice."

"And when you've finished with Bascombe you ought to talk to John Norton. President of Pilgrim Bank and Trust."

"Mrs. Drexel kept an account there?"

Jimmy Olsen laughed and slapped me on the shoulder. "You could put it that way, Mac. Mrs. Drexel owned the bank."

FIVE

"Sherry? Port?" the law-yer Bascombe Midgeley asked, offering, with an out-stretched arm, inspection of and selection from an oval silver tray which I thought to be a wedding gift from his grandparents if I read the inverted inscription correctly. On the tray were small, pear-shaped, leaded-crystal glasses and a selection of cocktail wines. "Harvey's Hunting Port? Chilly day. Might just hit the spot, old cock."

"The Hunting Port sounds fine, thank you."

"And just a spot of gin for me, I think." He poured for us and knocked his gin right down. It was noon, after all.

Jimmy Olsen was right, Bascombe Midgeley was full of himself. His was a barrister's office with oak-paneled walls which held shelves of leather-bound law books, an old red and blue Persian carpet of dubious origin, and a fireplace in which big chunks of cannel coal were burning. A gleam-ing brass banker's lamp with an emerald-green glass shade sat on an old oak desk. Prints of horses and sailing boats, hunting and racing scenes were hung on the walls. And on a small mahogany side table, in a smart silver frame, there was an autographed picture of Prince Philip taken at some lush, tropical locale. A nifty office all in all, small-town upscale.

"We met at an ecological conference in Bermuda," Bascombe Midgeley said, seeing that I had taken notice of the picture of the prince. "Nice chap really, when one gets to know him. Down to earth. Very interested in nature and preservation. He and I are like two peas in a pod, really."

"I've heard that about him. From others. I've never met him myself, needless to say."

"Very conservative, of course."

"Yes, I should imagine. Married to a queen and all."

He had not quite decided if I was being serious or putting him on. He crossed his legs, leaned his chin on his fist and scrutinized yours truly, with a hint of a twinkle in his eye. "Boston *Globe*, eh?" He held out his hand. "Credentials? Press card? Bona fides?"

"I'm just a temporary stringer. Call the *Globe* if you're concerned about my credentials. As I've told you, I want to talk to you about the Drexel will. And according to the papers I've just read in probate court over in Barnstable you were her lawyer. Am I correct?"

"Indeed, you are."

"It's a very interesting will. I'd like to talk to you about its implications."

Bascombe Midgeley was in his early thirties. He had a round face and straight, lifeless blond hair, brook-blue eyes, and he wore round eyeglasses with thin gold frames. He was dressed in a blue three-piece pinstripe suit, a blue button-down shirt, a rep striped bow tie and black Church's captoe shoes. A gold chain bearing a Phi Beta Kappa key was strung across his chest. He was a fairly young cat who looked as if he had dressed himself in his dead father's best clothes.

He stood and clasped his hands behind his back. Just like Prince Philip. Pursed his lips. "You've read the will. What's your impression?"

"My impression is that Jane Drexel left all her money,

every cent of it, to something called The North Walpole Trust. What does it say?—" I got out my notebook and read from it. " 'To be used for the preservation, beautification of and the cultural and social enhancement of life in North Walpole, Massachusetts, now and forevermore.' "

"*As!*"—Bascombe Midgeley pointed a finger to heaven—"as, McFarland."

" 'As the board of trustees sees fit to use it' is the way I would interpret it."

"Correct. A simple will really."

"Which you wrote and filed."

"Correct once again."

"And the trust?"

"Is not a public matter."

"Members of the board of trustees?"

"Again, not a public matter."

I stood. "Okay. If that's the way you want to read it in the *Globe* tomorrow morning, you got it. Thanks for your time and for the Hunting Port which was dry and nutty, just like you." Gee, it felt good to be back at work again.

"My dear chap, how very droll and so unexpected from one with your accent. But so many of you scribblers are that way, aren't you? Time for lunch, wouldn't you say?"

"If you'll be my guest."

"But of course. Delighted. Wouldn't have it any other way. Dry and nutty, indeed."

If you didn't want to sit at the counter at Bob's Sandwich Shop and try the meat-loaf special, which wasn't bad, the only other place in North Walpole to eat lunch in winter was the dining room at the Buckaneer, the one inn that stayed open year-round. It featured Early American decor and middle-aged waitresses who rolled their eyes and giggled when Bascombe Midgeley and I entered that day.

64

"My usual table, my dear girl," he said to the sixty-year-old hostess after he had shed himself of his lined Burberry. And, to the overweight waitress with the black wig who was struggling not to laugh in his face, "My usual aperitif." To me, "They all know me here, of course. What's your poison?"

"I'll just have a beer."

"Chop-chop," he said to the waitress. "And be quick about it."

Beefeater's on the rocks with a twist of lemon peel was his usual aperitif. He had three of them. After his second, he pulled a small enamel box from his vest pocket. "Lopressor, Aldomet, Lasix," he said, popping pills and washing them down with his gin.

"High blood pressure?"

"High enough." He took a drink. "Don't smoke though."

Bascombe Midgeley's wife, he informed me during lunch, was a terrific gal and a darn good sport. *Cape Cod Life* was planning a big spread next summer on the eighteenth-century house they had restored, adding a big addition, of course. His wife was a member of The Colonial Dames of America. His Harvard law-school classmates were all getting rich in New York, working themselves to death to be able to vacation where he lived year-round. Walter Cronkite, who summered over on Martha's Vineyard, was a nice guy and a good saltwater sailor. Ted Kennedy—agree with his politics or not, and he didn't—had really grown as a person since they had first met years ago.

I learned all this and more. He knocked down his gin, then ordered a bowl of chowder and the broiled scrod because he said he had to watch his weight. I told the waitress the same for me.

"I know what you're after, old cock," he said between bites. "You want to know how much money is in that trust."

"Well, everybody knows it's a lot. It seems to me you'll

65

save yourself a lot of headaches if you go public now and end all the speculation and gossip."

"We are, indeed, speaking of a fortune."

"Thirty? Am I close?"

"I knew somebody like you would show up. And you're right. Better to get the facts out and end all the rumors. But poor Jane Drexel was dear to me. She has been most foully murdered and I am anxious to avoid a damned carnival of thrills, if I can. The way Newport was during the von Bülow trial, with reporters and television cameras everywhere. Even *T-shirts!*"

"I can appreciate your concern. I hope it won't come to that." I decided, smug and full of himself, yes, but no fool, far from it, somebody to heed, somebody who had his own ornate way of conveying to you messages he wanted you to hear.

"So let's do display some restraint at our typewriter, shall we?" he said.

"I'll write it like Edith Wharton."

"That *is* the spirit, old cock. All right. Fifty. And change. And you didn't get any of this directly from me. No direct quotes."

I realized he had wanted to tell me the amount because I had been far too low in my estimate. "I can't even imagine that much money," I said. "You drew up the terms of the trust?"

"I did. With the assistance of a Wall Street firm. You see, except for a sizable amount of money she kept in our local bank for cash-flow purposes, almost all her fortune is invested. Jane Drexel left a stock and bond portfolio as thick as a Gutenberg Bible."

"Too much for you to handle yourself?"

"Oh, goodness, yes. You need tax specialists, accountants, a small army for something as complicated as this."

"Will it fly?"

"I would bet on it. It's carefully drawn. Well written. Thoroughly researched. And besides, old cock, who's going to challenge it? So far as we can determine she had no living relatives. We even hired detectives and a family-tree expert in Boston. No, just one old lady."

"I gather you're a North Walpole native."

"My father was a clergyman here."

"And you were Mrs. Drexel's attorney? On other matters as well, I mean."

"I was her lawyer here in North Walpole, yes. With that much money one tends to have lots of lawyers."

"You're also the executor of the will. It's brand new. That will is only four days old."

"Correct. That was the purpose of her trip here."

"In the dead of winter? Couldn't she have signed it at her winter home in Florida?"

"Of course she could have done so. And I so urged her. But old people often are funny when it comes to money. They get set in their ways. They want things done in certain ways and nothing else will do."

"And the will now sets the trust into existence."

"Correct, but don't try to make anything out of that. Until her death she was administering the trust herself, in a manner of speaking. You see, she loved our little town and she was determined to keep it exactly as it is. Unspoiled. And not become another Nantucket."

"I'm new here, Midgeley."

"Sky-high real estate prices, so high that common working people can barely afford to live there anymore. Nantucket has Texans who commute on weekends in the summer on private jets. And bring their decorators with them from Houston. She didn't want that."

"I see. I think I do, at least."

"She didn't want another Hyannis, either. Overdevelopment. High rises. Housing projects. She didn't want developers coming in here, making deals under the counter, buying up water-view land, property around the harbor and the ponds and building condos and marinas, no matter how well done."

"In the Midwest, where I come from, we call that progress."

"I know you do. People here have other ideas, some of us do. Jane Drexel, for one, certainly did."

"New construction's going up all around here. Who are you trying to kid? It looks like a population explosion."

"Oh, there is no way anybody can stop it. All she was trying to do was contain it, channel it. So when any attractive piece of land came on the market, she just outbid everybody else and bought it. She had the money to do it, after all."

"I don't know. People got a right to live anywhere they like, providing they can afford it. This is a democracy, right?"

"Unfortunately, yes." He smiled. "At least Princess Jane would have looked at it that way. She would have much preferred a benevolent monarchy. With herself as queen of state, it goes without saying. Nice little half Capes to live in and Christmas turkeys for everyone."

"You didn't like her."

"I loved her."

"It's not the same thing. What did she do with all the land she bought?"

"She gave it to the preservation society."

"And you were the one who did the buying and the giving away, all the legal work?"

"Correct. The payments, the actual transfer of funds, were always handled by John Norton, who's president of Pilgrim Bank and Trust."

"Mrs. Drexel's bank."

"Most of it. There are minor stockholders. I'm one. So is Johnny. Six or seven others. Local businessmen. But she owned most of the stock and, of course, was by far the largest depositor."

"She wanted quick access to ready money when she wanted to buy land."

"Correct."

"And now that she's dead, the trust takes over. With a lot of money to throw around. Millions a year from dividends and interest payments. To be spent any way the trustees see fit. Who's on the board besides you?"

"Who says I am? Carrot cake and coffee, please," he called to the waitress with the black wig. "But, yes, I am. A trustee as well as general counsel."

"Which means a retainer."

"Only fair. Lots of work. I'll not tell you how much. I will tell you that Mrs. Drexel set the figure, not I."

"Who else?"

"A moment please." He was forking into the carrot cake, which didn't look bad.

"John Norton, of course. Bank president. That figures."

"Yes. And Mrs. Harrison Bingham. She's executive director of the preservation society. Kate, her name is."

"Just you three?"

He slammed his fork down. "Damn it all, McFarland. You are a most persistent person, to the point of being more than a bit annoying. Especially when one is trying to down one's carrot cake with fresh whipped cream."

"Damn it, Midgeley, I've got a deadline to meet and I've got a lot of other people I must see."

"And I don't give a fig for your deadline." He ate the last of his cake. "Noah Simmons. No doubt you two have met."

"The police chief."

"And a marine biologist. Don't forget that. Not a bad choice when you consider it. Mrs. Drexel knew what she was doing. You see, we have a most fragile ecological balance out here. We're a peninsula, after all, sticking right out in the North Atlantic like a cocked arm. And we've had a growth explosion during the last twenty years. We have water-table problems, pollution problems. This place can hold only so many people, and Noah's an expert on it. A good choice."

"So you four are going to hand out the goodies. You're going to be four very big fish in this little pond."

"Whales, old cock. Not just big fish. Whales."

"Looking forward to it?"

"Clergymen don't get paid very well on the Cape, McFarland. At least my father didn't. He clerked part time in the hardware store on Main Street to make extra money. I grew up poor and I will admit the temptation is there."

"To lord it over the town?"

"I said the *temptation* is there. But I shall not give in to it. I am determined to be just and fair. With the exception of four or five miserable sons of bitches I will not name."

I paid, got a signed receipt, and Bascombe Midgeley and I got our coats and left the Buckaneer. The cold air on Main Street felt good on my face.

"You really are not a very good reporter, are you, old cock? An easy touch," he said.

"What do you mean?"

"You never asked if there is another one. Another trustee. And there *is*, a fifth one, but I haven't even had the chance to tell him yet. For some reason Mrs. Drexel didn't want him to know until after her death. A retired schoolteacher who's summered for years in a little cottage on the edge of her property. His name is Gerald Dickerson."

"Gerald Dickerson?" I was stunned.

70

"Nice old man. Good day, old cock." And with a slight bow and a sardonic salute with the gloves he was holding, he was gone.

I found Noah Simmons in his office, just four blocks down the street from the Buckaneer. It was midafternoon and he looked like hell, no shave, same clothes, and apparently no sleep the night before. The coffee he was drinking was of the color and viscosity of coal tar. "How was the scrod and the carrot cake, old cock?" he asked.

"Have you got the whole town wired?"

"I was driving down Main. I saw the two of you going in for lunch. Bascombe always has the scrod and carrot cake. How many pops?"

"Four, counting the one in his office."

"He drinks too damn much."

"Doesn't smoke, though. And speaking of physical fitness, you'd better get a hot meal in your stomach. Go home, get in a shower. And get some sleep. You don't look too good."

He stood up, stretched, yawned, a bear in winter. "You know, you're right. Come on."

I didn't ask any questions. We rode up Main Street in his white Ford Fairlane patrol car. The town looked almost deserted. The street was heavily salted and free of snow, and runoff water was gurgling in the gutters. But the yards were still covered.

"There's something you ought to know," I said. "I got a job stringing for the *Globe*. Any objections?"

"No. I figured that might be what the phone call was about. I guess that makes us natural adversaries, as they say."

"That's not the way I like to work. I got no ax to grind. I'll do my best to work with you, not against you."

"If it turns out that way it'll be the first time." Which is what they usually said.

We rode past the North Walpole lighthouse, which stands on a bluff, overlooking the North Atlantic, and where there is a small Coast Guard station. The ocean was clear blue, dead cold. No wind to speak of and no warning flag flying from the halyard.

Noah rubbed his eyes. "My problem is I haven't had any sleep for *two* nights running. Night before last it was a family problem, my first cousin and her husband."

"I met your cousin's husband at probate this morning. Jimmy Olsen."

"You know that little guy beats the hell out of her. Not on any regular basis, just when she pushes him too far. Delores can be pushy at times."

"He told me he runs his home like Patton."

"Well, let's say he tries. They got into it night before last and I was up most of the night trying to quiet them down."

"From the picture he showed me, she looks big enough to take care of herself."

"The problem is they love each other, crazy about each other. Always have been, except when they're fighting. And it's not one-sided. Now and then she'll bide her time, wait until he's not expecting it and hit him for something he did or said weeks before. Broke his jaw once."

We both laughed. Hey, I was beginning to feel like an old North Walpolean. Another sixty or seventy years of living and working here and these people might start accepting me as one of their own. No guarantee of it, of course.

Noah turned off the main road and drove down a narrow lane which ended at a strip of sand. It was a little harbor beach. He cut the engine and we got out. Colder on the water. He took a series of deep breaths, which was sort of like watching the Goodyear blimp being inflated and deflated. He walked down to the edge of the water, dipped his hands in and bathed his face. Pilgrim Harbor was not frozen but small chunks of ice were floating in the water.

"It's a little cove," he said. "Small craft anchor here in the summer. Water here is filled with them, catboats, all sorts of day sailers. I used to keep one here myself when I was a kid. Also the beach along here is full of clams and mussels. Dig them up with your hands if you know the right spots. I put beach patrols here in the summer. We ticket you if you don't have your license, and I mean pinned on so it's visible, or if we catch you exceeding the limit of one bucket a day."

"I like it here, Noah."

"Ah, it's the best place on earth to live." He started undressing. Honest to God, started taking off his clothes and laying them on the hood of his car. Wearing just his shorts, he ran out and launched himself, creating waves that made you think about a Poseidon submarine being commissioned. Noah Simmons was taking a bath.

"Look at a map," he called to me when he surfaced. "You'll see you are standing right smack in the North Atlantic Ocean, my friend."

Floating on his back now. "You like wildlife? Nature? The Cape is on an Atlantic flyway. All kinds of birds. Osprey. Peregrine falcons. Herons, ducks, geese. Now and then even a bald eagle. Animals, deer, foxes, skunks, you name it."

He did a nice, powerful breaststroke, swam about fifty yards out, then swam back with a crawl, submerged, surfaced and blew like a whale, and finally waded out, all three hundred pounds of him.

"Want to talk fish? Fluke, scup, weakfish, tautog, sea bass, blues, flounder, not to mention cod, except you got to go

73

out to the banks to get them. Whales? You can see them surface. Little harbor seals. They come down from Nova Scotia."

He opened the trunk of his patrol car where he kept towels and a jogging suit. He dried his hair, rubbed down his body and started dressing. "Berries? Black, blue, elder, straw. Wild cranberries. Wild beach plums in the fall. They make the best jelly in the world." He combed his hair with his fingers. "Boy, do I feel better." He looked it. We got back in the car and he started the engine and turned on the heater.

"I checked you out. Just like you said, no record. In fact, there were some pretty nice things said about you."

"Will you be wanting a deposition or anything like that?"

"We'll see." He paused. "I went back to the cottage late last night after your lights were off. I went through that place from top to bottom. There was nothing there. What did Mr. Dickerson think was in there? He was dying to get inside."

"Money. Ten thousand dollars. In his refrigerator." I told him the story.

"Hell, we all knew she was helping him out. No secrets in this town, damn few anyway. But there was no money there that I could see. The refrigerator was disconnected, door wide open. And empty."

"You said you found the refrigerator in the main house open, with food scattered all over the floor. Mr. Dickerson vows Mrs. Drexel was playing with a deck of forty-six, forty-seven cards for the past year or so. Maybe she had the money there, not at the cottage. And whoever killed her found it."

"Could be."

"Autopsy completed?"

"Yeah."

"Well? Want to tell McFarland of the *Globe* what's in it?"

"No stroke, no heart attack, no sexual entry, which is to say no rape. She didn't freeze to death. She was strangled. And the crime lab guys say there is evidence to indicate she was strangled inside the house and then dragged outside. By somebody who then took off. They found heel marks where she was dragged."

"If he had had her key he could have let himself back in."

"She had combination locks, Mac. Push-button jobs. Had them installed because she kept losing her keys."

"Then how did you get in?"

"Because I know the combination."

"A crazy? Somebody on drugs? No, because it stands to reason she knew the person well enough to let him in."

"I think she knew the person who killed her. I think I do, too. Nobody from out of town, I mean. But a lot of things simply do not make sense to me."

We were heading back into town. Noah yawned. "You're right, McFarland. I need sleep. I'm going to conk off this afternoon. Between you and me I've never handled anything like this before."

"I can't see that you made any glaring mistakes yet."

"No, I don't think so. The forensic team will have a full report for me in two or three days on tracks, fibers, prints. I got police locks on all the doors. Police presence at the house round the clock. No evidence I know of has been tampered with. And we've checked around. No strangers in town we can't account for."

"Could that trust she set up somehow be involved in all this? You're talking big bucks there."

"The thought has struck me. But I don't see how."

"All five of you on the board of trustees have known each other for a long time, haven't you?"

"Sure. The four of us grew up here together. Not close friends then, especially, but we all knew each other. You know everybody in North Walpole when you live here. Me, Bascombe, John and Kate. But we really didn't get to know each other that well until Mr. Dickerson tutored us the summer before we all went off to college at Mrs. Drexel's expense.

"What year was that?"

"The summer of seventy-one." He smiled at the memory. "I have never had so much stuffed into my head so quickly before or since. And, you know, a lot of it has stuck."

"Do you have any idea why the four of you were chosen?"

"She never said."

"Police chief, banker, lawyer, preservation society director. You could almost make the case that Mrs. Drexel got just what she set out to get, a handpicked group to run her little town after she was gone. I hadn't realized Mrs. Bingham was your contemporary, though. I imagined an older person. Bridge-club type."

"You obviously have not met Katey," Noah said.

I hurried back to the house after I left Noah Simmons, knowing full well that I was in big trouble. Just didn't want to admit it to myself. There was still plenty of time to make a six o'clock deadline. Any halfway competent reporter can write a paperback novel in a couple of hours.

And I had a reputation as a fast, adequate writer. What was it A. J. Liebling said about himself? Anybody who can write faster than I can, I can write better than he can. And anybody who can write better than I can, I can write faster than he can. That about summed it up.

I got my old reliable portable Olivetti out of the hall closet, knowing I was uptight. Placed it on the coffee table in the living room and rolled a sheet of typing paper into it, knowing full well that I was terrified. And sat there and stared at it, just as I had known I would. Stared at my notes. Stared at the typewriter, at the fire, at the dog, stared out the window.

A lead paragraph was what I needed, and I have rapped out thousands of them. Usually they pop into your head. A reporter not being able to write a lead paragraph upon call is like a doctor not knowing how to take your blood pressure. It's basic.

A good, crisp lead—I always tried to keep them to three lines of type—and the rest of the story just follows for me, bang, bang, bang, as fast as I can type, no matter how complicated the subject matter. That was how I made my living. My problem that afternoon, and I knew this but that didn't help, was that I wanted to knock Dave Farkas's socks off with this first story, show him that I was indeed still Mr. World Class. Wanted the downtown Boston bankers and the professors in Cambridge and the young reporters in the city room at the *Globe* to read my words, whistle in admiration and say, "Who is this guy? He can really write. Fresh styling. Deft phrasing. Tremendous organization. Reads almost like a short story." It was very important to me. So I sat there and kept staring at the typewriter.

Oh, Muse, you bitch, give me a break, will you? I got up and walked around the room, tried that. Write something, anything. I tried half a dozen leads and threw them all away. Three o'clock, four o'clock, five o'clock rock. The first writer's block I had ever experienced. Just not that fancy with my fingers. Get it down.

At five-fifteen, sweating like a field hand, I grabbed my notebook, jumped in the car and drove hell for leather into town. There was a phone booth on one corner of the Texaco station at the bottom of Main Street. I dialed the *Globe* collect and asked for dictation. You see, a world-class deadline reporter such as I should be able to dictate acceptable copy from notes as well as write it. With practice it's not as hard as you might think. That was what I had come down to, publish or perish.

"Go ahead, please. The tape is rolling and I am monitoring," the *Globe* dictationist said. I just stood there. For the first time in my life I was going to miss a deadline. Choked up.

"Sir?"

Couldn't speak. Mouth dry. Gasping for breath. World class.

"Sir? Are you there? My tape is rolling."

Say something. I said nothing.

"*Look*, asshole! You think I got all day? Start *talking!*" the dictationist screamed. Instant therapy.

I opened my mouth and words came.

Slug McFarland slant murder. Paragraph. Jane Drexel comma, D-R-E-X-E-L comma, an old widow comma, rich and generous comma, loved this little Cape Cod village period. And most people here returned that affection period. With one notable and mysterious exception period. Somebody here strangled the Boston-born heiress to death last Monday night period paragraph.

SIX

I DROVE DIRECTLY TO THE
Binnacle as soon as I had finished dictating the story, got
the last open seat at the bar and gulped down whiskey until
my feeling of panic had subsided and some sense of self-
confidence slowly returned. After two drinks I told myself,
Well, you did it, wrote the story. No masterpiece, no prize
winner, but acceptable copy. Made the deadline. Tomorrow you can talk to Dave Farkas man to man. And maybe
it'll read better in print. Usually does.

"You got three more minutes until happy hour prices
end. *Sir*," the bar waitress said.

"A double," I said handing, her my empty glass.

The Binnacle Bar and Grill had stained pine walls, scarred
tables and a beer-soaked red-and-gold carpet. There were
a couple of stuffed Canadian geese and a medium-sized
swordfish mounted on the walls. Nothing fancy, goodness
knows. But there was a real fireplace, a big one, and—the
Binnacle's greatest virtue—it was the only bar in North
Walpole that stayed open year-round.

The waitress poured me a bomb, spewed on a little soda
from the nozzle, and placed it in front of me on the bar.
Its color matched the stained pine walls. "Big fellow like
you should be able to handle this with *no* problem," she

said. "I'm Mary Beth. Drink up and I may be able to sneak you another one half price."

She was just a kid, but a kid with breasts the size of 1942 LaSalle headlights and a head of long, straight auburn hair that fell down to the small of her back. A big child destined one day to be a huge momma, although the eventuality of a half dozen kids hanging on to her like crabs on a chicken neck was still a few years off. She was dressed in tight, faded jeans and a sweatshirt. TRY IT YOU'LL LIKE IT! said the sweatshirt.

A dude with a beard and a potbelly, obviously the manager, commanded the main portion of the bar, including the section where the floor waitresses placed their table orders. There was a big happy hour crowd and he was a busy man. "On the house, Katey," he said, placing a drink before the woman sitting next to me.

"Thanks, Nickey."

"Sorry to hear about the old lady."

"How tall are you, anyhow?" Mary Beth asked me. "Six-two? Six-three?"

"Something like that."

"I like tall guys. My dad's a twerp."

"How old are you, Mary Beth?"

"Twenty-one. Just turned. Look at this." She did a left face, sucked in her breath and pulled out the waist of her jeans. "Not bad, huh? I swore to God I'd get down to one thirty by my twenty-first birthday, and I did it. You should have seen me before. I won't tell you how much I weighed. Even under torture."

"I was thinking your face looks a little familiar. Your last name wouldn't be Olsen, would it?"

"How'd you know that? That's weird."

"I've got a memory for faces, for some reason. I know your dad, slightly. And your uncle Noah."

"Then you know I was a fat kid. Dad show you the family

80

photo he keeps in his office? He shows it to everybody. I was the blob in the middle." She leaned over the bar and whispered to me. "Now everybody in town wants to screw me."

"I can imagine."

"I never had any experience handling it before, you know?"

"When's the funeral?" the bearded bartender asked the blond woman sitting next to me.

"Tomorrow morning at eleven. Saint Matt's." She was a fairly tall woman. She wore eyeglasses which were tipped forward on her nose and she was dressed in jeans, a thick white sweater and a red down vest.

"Absolute happy hour deadline in ten seconds," Mary Beth said. "Ten, nine, eight . . ."

"Another one for me and one for my bar companion here."

The woman didn't look at me but neither did she push the drink away when Mary Beth served it to her. Then Mary Beth leaned over to whisper to me again. "When I said I never had any experience handling it, what I mean is absolutely *noooo* experience. Know what I mean? How to say no, for example."

"That could be a problem. I can see that."

"You just don't learn those things when you're a fat teenage blob. For instance, I always thought the bigger the guy the bigger the wang, you know?"

I lit a cigarette only to notice I already had two others burning in the ashtray.

"Like you I would have figured would have one as long as your arm. And maybe you do, for all I know," Mary Beth said.

I also had two drinks lined up on the bar before me, one the color of stained pine and the latest one the color of Harry Belafonte.

"Like that horse," Mary Beth said. "Remember some

king or somebody gave the President that horse as a present and it was on live television on the White House lawn and this horse had this *huge* hard on? I was home in bed with the flu watching and I almost fainted. The size of that thing, Jesus Christ!"

"Mary Beth!" It almost was a scream coming from the woman next to me. Then, less frantic, "You have a customer waving at you at the end of the bar."

"Candid youngster," I said as she walked away.

"Been that way all her life. Totally obsessed by sex. You never know what she's going to say next because she doesn't either."

"I had a wife once who was a lot like that."

"You're the one who found Jane Drexel, aren't you?"

"Yes, I am. My name's McFarland."

"You fit the description. Noah Simmons told me about you."

"And unless I miss my guess, you're Kate Bingham. I've been listening to you talk with the bartender. I'm a newspaperman, Mrs. Bingham, and I'm working for the Boston *Globe*. You might as well know. I'm on this story."

Her face flushed. "Why don't you people just leave us alone? We're just small-town yokels here, you know."

I shrugged my shoulders. "Nothing personal. I needed a job and one got offered to me."

She had green eyes, this Kate Bingham did, and a few faint freckles spread in a line across her nose. And a long neck. No makeup. And I know that doesn't sound like much, so I should add that Mrs. Harrison Bingham was not a "pretty" woman. She was a beautiful woman. Hers was a classically beautiful face one woman in a million is born with. With a face like that, growing up with it as a kid, frowning at it in the mirror, and finally realizing what you've got, you don't have to worry too much about makeup.

You got a face like that, at her age, you know it, how could you not?

"You know, you sort of look like a giraffe," I told her. "I mean that as a compliment, believe it or not. To me, I mean, a giraffe is a beautiful animal."

She looked me over. "How much have you had to drink?"

A little too much. I raised my glass. " 'Wild nights! Wild nights! Were I with thee, Wild nights should be our luxury!' " That drew a smile. "I learned it in college. I had to write a term paper on her. That's the only poem by her I know."

It worked. "My name's Kate," she said.

"I know. I was going to give you a call tomorrow, sometime after the funeral. I'd like to talk to you about the North Walpole trust Mrs. Drexel created. Maybe you and Mr. Bingham, if he's free. Is he a businessman or what?"

The happy hour crowd was beginning to clear out, the same crowd, more or less, that showed up at Bob's Sandwich Shop every morning. Mary Beth, I noticed, was at the far end of the bar, chatting it up with a guy who had bad news written all over his face. And pointing at me.

"You got a first name by any chance?" Kate Bingham asked.

"I think it's Mudd," I said because this mean-looking guy was heading for me, fire in his eye.

"Kate, you oughtn't to be associating with his sort," he said. "Because this is an asshole."

I knew I was in trouble. Subtle, but I got the drift.

"Rocko, can't you see this gentleman and I are having a private conversation?" Kate said, and a good try, too.

"You fucker," Rocko said to me. Rocko was, shall we say, drunk as a dog.

"A literary conversation. Nothing a fisherman would be interested in," Kate told him.

"Oh? You a fisherman, Rocko?" I asked.

"Rocko's drunk is what Rocko is," Kate said. "Married and three beautiful kids and still trying to lay every woman in town over the age of fourteen. He's been trying to lay me since high school when he was the star halfback. Haven't you, Rocko? Now he's making a play for little Mary Beth. You'll get there one of these days, Rocko, if you keep trying."

"Well, it's nice to meet you, Rocko," I said. His name would have to be Rocko, wouldn't it?

Mary Beth had ambled over to get a ringside view. "You little slut!" Kate snapped at her. Mary Beth giggled.

"Kate, this guy here's been telling Mary Beth what a big cock he's got. Nice young girl like her don't have to listen to crap like that, even from a paying customer."

"Rocko, this gentleman happens to be a very cultured person who can quote Emily Dickerson."

"Kate, will you please shut the hell up?" I said.

"He told me it was big as a horse's," Mary Beth said. "I don't know wild animals. Just dogs and cats."

"You know Emily Dickerson, don't you, Rocko?" Kate said.

"Who is this Emily Dickerson? She from around here?" This is what Rocko said to me.

"She was a poet. You dumb Irish Catholic son of a bitch," Kate said to Rocko.

"Nobody calls me that," Rocko said to me.

"Wait a minute! I didn't call you anything."

"He told me it was as big as the President of the United States' horse's," Mary Beth said. She was the sort of little liar who started promoting fights over her honor in grade school.

"You come in here using foul language before a minor and then make fun of my faith," Rocko said.

"Oh, Rocko, just cold-cock him," Mary Beth said airily,

84

which is what Rocko did, which is what he had been planning to do all along. I was slow on the uptake, should have
seen it coming sooner. I paid for it, too.

He was quick and strong, an experienced street fighter,
and, worst of all, a guy who *liked* to fight. His idea of a fun
night out. He hit me twice in the face, left, right, hooked
me hard in my gut twice, then, before I had any chance
to even think about putting my own act together, hoisted
me up, kneed me in the balls, and shoved me through the
picture window of The Binnacle Bar and Grill.

It hurt, hurt more than my pride. I landed on my back
on the Main Street sidewalk, beside the entrance, sending
a shower of broken glass in all directions. I mean, can't you
just see me lying there, fifty years old? The good news was
that I was viable and conscious; the bad news was that I
was at least twenty years older than young Rocko and in
terrible physical condition.

My general operating rule always has been, never mess
around when you find yourself in a situation such as this.
Don't think, don't try to make a plan, *act*, do something,
almost anything, because when the Rockos of this world
come at you, the issue usually is beyond further discussion.

There was a cord of firewood neatly stacked beside the
entrance of the Binnacle, let me tell you a beautiful sight.
I grabbed a stick of it and met Rocko when he threw open
the door and rushed out, breathing fire, wanting some
more of me. Thank God he was drunk. I swung for the
BENRUS sign over center field, swung the way a Class A
batting coach once had taught me, and hit Rocko squarely
in the face.

He fell backward, his feet sliding from under him, but
then so did I when I tried to hit him again. The weather
had changed abruptly; it was sleeting and the sidewalk,
cleared earlier of the snow, had become covered with a

thin sheet of ice. The fight, so-called, became a slipping, sliding wrestling match until a bunch of other guys who had piled out of the bar to see the action pulled and held us apart.

Mary Beth was jumping up and down like a cheerleader screaming "Yeaaaa!"

I pulled free, placed my back against the side of a car parked at the curb, and waited for whatever was going to happen next. My face was throbbing from Rocko's best shots and the nicks and cuts from my trip through the window were burning. Jesus! Did you enjoy your stay on the Cape? Aren't the people there friendly and easy to get to know? And so many cozy little bars and restaurants, getaways.

Rocko's nose was bleeding. He tried to come at me again but three of his friends held him in tow. "Get him out of here," Kate ordered them. "Take him to the boat and sober him up. And be sure and call Paulette and explain." They dragged him off, down the street, and the other customers went back inside the bar.

"You didn't call the cops, did you?" Kate asked Nickey the bartender who had come outside to inspect the damage.

"I'm just about to."

"Oh, come on."

"Kate, I could lose my license. And who is this guy, please? What exactly have I got on my hands here?"

"A friend of mine, Nickey."

"He's been in a few times. I noticed him. See, you know, Kate, I try to run a pleasant place here where people can come and relax, enjoy themselves, have a few pops. We don't want no troublemakers, you know that."

"It wasn't his fault, Nickey. He didn't throw himself through the window. You know Rocko."

"See, it's not just the damage, which is extremely extensive. There is also my reputation in this town, which I have to maintain."

"It's not the first fight at the Binnacle."

"See, but this is the first time I ever lost a window. Think of the business I'm going to lose. Customers don't want to sit in no cold bar and drink, not this time of year. They want a nice, warm bar, fire going. Cozy, you know."

"I'll pay you for the cost of replacing the window plus a hundred bucks for loss of business," I said.

"Now, see, this gentleman knows the proper way to act in a situation like this," Nickey said to Kate. "Plus lettering. THE BINNACLE BAR AND GRILL. And under that a new word. SEAFOOD. I want tourists next summer to know the place ain't just for hamburgers."

"Plus Seafood."

"He'll pay for half the cost of replacing the window. You can damn well make Rocko kick in for the rest," Kate said.

Nickey considered it, shrugged his shoulders. "So get him out of here, Kate. Call in tomorrow I'll give you an estimate. I'll tell Noah it was an accident."

"You think you need to see a doctor?" Kate asked me.

"No."

"Come on, then. I'm going to drive you home."

"Please don't. I've known people like you. Trouble seeks you out."

"Just shut up and come on. I don't have all night." Kate, as I was to learn all too well, had a way of cutting through to the heart of things.

"Sweet Jesus! Are you telling me that an actual person, an actual human being lives in this dump?" That was her reaction when she got her first look at my digs.

"I'm just house-sitting. I didn't decorate the joint."

She walked slowly around the living room, inspecting it,

her mouth open in feigned wonder. The old hot plate on the mantel. The vast, widely distributed collection of dirty glasses and coffee cups. The unmade bed. The pile of dirty laundry. The two-week stack of newspapers. MouMou's matted sheepskin nightnight. The whole scene.

"I mean, come on. Knock off that opened-mouth-in-amazement act. It's a little messy, I admit, but it's not that bad."

"Yes, it is. It's that bad." She hugged herself. "And furthermore, it is freezing in here. Is the heat turned off?"

First day on the new job and all, I had forgotten to call the furnace repairman and the big fire I had left for MouMou had burned down to a few faint coals. I wadded some sheets of newspaper and threw them on and stacked a new rack of wood on top. The fire smoked briefly, then caught. Felt good, too. We both warmed ourselves before it.

The ride home from the Binnacle, only a couple of miles, had been a winter adventure. What appeared to be a mixture of sleet, snow and freezing rain was falling heavily and the plowed roads were as slick as an Olympic toboggan run. We slipped and slid all the way to the old house, narrowly missing ditches, trees and hedges, with Kate, who had had one drink too many and didn't realize it, screaming and cursing at the top of her lungs as she maneuvered her Toyota. Somehow we had made it.

The policeman on duty in the patrol car parked in the Drexel driveway got out when he spotted our approaching headlights on the dark road but made no move to stop us when we turned into the driveway of the Hollings place next door. We slid down the driveway to the house, sure in the knowledge that the car would never make it out again, not that night, not without the aid of a wrecker.

So here we were, beautiful Kate Bingham and I. "You are a bloody mess, McFarland," she declared. "Rocko's nose bled all over your coat and you ought to see your face. You got any iodine? Band-Aids? And I suppose hot water is too much to expect in this—this *place*."

There was an old first-aid box hanging on the wall in the kitchen which looked like a relic from World War II. I got it, along with a saucepan of water which I placed on the hot plate. "Be gentle with me," I said.

"I'm pretty good at this actually. Learned at my mother's knee. She's a registered nurse." She was feeling my head with her hands. "You know, you're not bad looking actually. Not good looking, but not bad looking either. Except your face is pretty puffy where old Rocko let you have it. How old are you?"

"Thirty-five."

"Liar. You are a liar! Do you hurt anywhere in your body? Feel funny anywhere? Let me see you twist your head and move your neck." She bathed my cuts and nicks with warm water, dabbed them with iodine and stuck a couple of small plastic bandages here and there. "How do you feel?"

"Exactly like somebody punched me out and threw me through a picture window."

"Teach you to talk dirty to young girls."

I looked around the room. "I guess you're right. I could use a cleaning woman."

"A cleaning woman? You need a bulldozer."

"I guess I've sort of let it get out of control."

"Class. You are strictly a class act, McFarland. And what exactly is *that*?" MouMou had come about halfway out from under the couch.

"It's a dog, more or less. She hates my guts."

"No wonder, leaving her here all day long in a freezing house. You mean that thing actually is your dog?"

"It's a long story."

89

I built up the fire until it looked like the inside of the boiler furnace of a medium-size Amazon riverboat and it almost but not quite warmed the room. Kate and I sat on the couch and watched it burn, sat there for a few minutes without talking. A lot had happened, after all.

"You with anybody?" I asked. I had gotten no feedback at the Binnacle when I had asked about Mr. Bingham.

"No."

"I mean . . ."

"I know what you mean. No. And what business is it of yours?"

"None. Sorry I asked." A tough one. I decided to change the subject. "What in the world are you people going to do with all that money Jane Drexel left in the trust?"

"Spend it. What else?"

"We're talking about annual interest on about fifty million dollars, as I understand it. You're going to be a very powerful person in this community with all that cash to scatter around."

"Jane and I were very close, Mac. And she had very definite ideas about how she wanted her money spent. We had long talks about it."

"Such as?"

"None of your business, really, but, well, the trust might buy this place, for example."

"This dump? Surely you joke."

"You're new here. You don't know Cape Cod very well yet. This dump sits on over six acres of prime waterfront property. On Clam Pond, on salt water. Do you have any idea what it's worth?"

"I didn't even know what Cape Cod *was* until Noah and Bascombe explained it to me today."

"Around two hundred thousand dollars an acre is what it's worth. You're sitting on a million-dollar-plus piece of land."

"I find that hard to believe."

"Believe it. On a clear day you can almost see Nantucket. Until only a few years ago North Walpole was just a sleepy little Cape Cod town. You couldn't even find the place off Route Six unless you looked hard."

"That's still pretty much the case, it seems to me. I ended up here entirely by accident. Just driving. It's hard to find."

"Well, while North Walpole slept on, most of the rest of the Cape was being developed. High rises and condos and marinas all over the place, hotels and shopping centers. Prices have gone out of sight. You can pay half a million dollars for a little three-bedroom house on Nantucket and not even be close to the water."

"And now those prices have jumped over the Sound to North Walpole."

"Exactly. Land values are exploding here. You can't imagine. And the developers are circling this poor little town like a school of sharks. A developer could make a fortune if he could get his hands on this piece of property. With one-acre zoning in this part of town he could get six houses on it. At a half million each, at least."

"What would *you* do with it?"

"Maybe a park, maybe one with a public dock for small boats. Or maybe nothing. Tear this old house down and let the land sit here. The Cape already is overdeveloped. It's important that we leave some parts of it alone."

"Sometimes land gets so valuable you can't do that, no matter how nice it would be."

"I know. It's going to be a fight. I bitch and moan about this town a lot. But I love it with all my heart, the way it looks and smells, just *is*. And I'm going to do what I can to keep it from being destroyed. Especially now that Jane has left me with the means to do it."

That was when MouMou made her bid. She came twisting and nodding over to Kate, ready to jump into her lap at the hint of a smile. "Get!" Kate said authoritatively. "When I'm ready to deal with *you* I'll let you know." MouMou bowed her head in defeat and half crawled away.

"Good for you. High time she had a little negative reaction from somebody besides me. So for starters you want the trust to use some money and make a bid on this place?"

"Yes. Jane was very positive about it, ready to go. The problem is, the Hollings heirs are scattered all over. One is somewhere in the South Seas, I gather. It's very complicated. Johnny Norton runs the bank here. He's trying to run them all down and work up a deal."

"Kate, you do know that Mrs. Drexel was strangled, don't you? Murdered."

"Yes. Noah told me this afternoon."

"Have you got any theory about it at all?"

"Not really, no. I can't even imagine it happening. I guess I really haven't made myself think about it yet."

"Did she ever talk to you about being in danger? About feeling threatened? Anything like that? Anything that made you think *of course* when you learned about her death? Older people, especially if they are strong-willed, can get themselves into the damnedest situations because they refuse to recognize the fact that they've grown old."

"Danger? Jane? No." She smiled at the thought of Jane Drexel being afraid of anything or anybody.

"How did you two get so tight? As I understand it, she put you through college."

"Undergraduate and graduate school. You're looking at a Harvard Ph.D. when you gaze into these baby blues, friend."

"But how did she pick up on you? Were you the smartest kid in town going away, or what? Episcopal supergirl?"

"Episcopal? You got to be kidding. Katherine Mary O'Doul. You're looking at Irish Catholic, McFarland. I went from Saint John's nursery through high school all parochial. Wearing plaid jumpers and green blazers and white blouses. All uniforms, nuns and priests. Until I left for college I never attended a school that wasn't named for one saint or another."

"Still in the Church?"

"In it but not of it. I seldom go to Mass anymore. Although I did slip in today at noon. Sat way in the back, just me and the old scared women."

"Praying for Mrs. Drexel?"

"Well, there was nobody else."

"You loved that old woman, didn't you?"

"Yes, I did. We spent a lot of time together. I guess I was a sort of pet. She had no children of her own. She taught me a lot. I stood up to her, mind you. Never took any of her crap, and could she dish it out! Yes, I loved her."

"And she loved you, I bet. It must be like losing a member of the family."

Was there a tear in her eye? "I don't really know why she chose me. My mom, I think. I told you she's a nurse. She worked for Jane as a personal nurse through some illness when I was a little kid. Jane's husband, I think, who was dying. All I know is that a week after high school graduation I found myself at Mr. Dickerson's summer cottage right over there next door, studying my ass off all day long."

"He must have been tough. Noah says the same thing."

"He was an absolute tyrant. It was hard work but it was great fun, too, like being a member of a special club. And Jane was fun, like a housemother. She took a real interest in all four of us. She laid out a huge lunch for us every day. And in the afternoons, when classes were over, we'd all go swimming off the dock. Jane, too, and Mr. Dickerson.

It truly was a special summer, like a dream. Everybody was so damn happy."

"Then you were off to college?"

"To Wellesley. *Wellesley*. We had a college guidance counselor in high school who wanted me to apply to some little Catholic women's colleges I'd never even heard of. But Jane went to Wellesley and her parents had given the school about a thousand tons of money, I gather. All I know is I was accepted. 'Oh, my dear, good for you. You're going to Wellesley. It's all been arranged.' I remember Jane telling me that toward the end of that summer. I didn't even know I'd applied, just signed what she gave me to sign."

"No more plaid jumpers and green blazers?"

She smiled. "Also my last nun. I studied history. And later at Harvard, urban planning."

"With Jane Drexel's constant advice and attention all the way, I bet."

"Oh, yes. She was like that, at least with me. She wanted to know about every course I was taking. Everything."

"I really think she handpicked you four to carry on for her in North Walpole and trained you for it. That's the way it seems to me, more and more."

"I guess. That could be the case. I never thought about it that way."

"I would bet anything she guided you into the job you've got now, running the preservation society."

"That's true, she did."

"You are . . . Mrs. Bingham." I wanted to get things straight.

"That is correct," she said. "You are actually cuddled up here on this couch with a widow lady, McFarland."

"You can't be more than thirty years old."

"Thirty-one." She reached over and pulled at one of my earlobes. "McFarland, your ears stick out slightly. I guess you know that. Ever think about having them pinned back? It's a simple operation. You sort of look like Howdy Doody."

"Come on, Kate."

"Oh, he was a nice, sweet guy and I was crazy about him. A Californian who started out wanting to be a painter, and he wasn't a bad one. We met at Cambridge, spent the better part of a year together, got our doctorates the same day at Harvard and got married a month later. Mom's just got a small house so Jane insisted we use hers for the reception. Nice reception. Nice wedding at Saint John's. Harrison was a . . . a pilot. And like I told you, he was a Californian."

"You don't have to tell me about it. The truth is, I don't want to hear. I'm sorry I asked, okay?"

"An amateur pilot and, well, a little bit of a showoff. He was from Newport Beach, California. Not obnoxious. Not at all. Just full of himself, you know? You must know people like that in your business. You can't get angry at people like Harrison."

The fire was dying down and there was no more wood in the house. I felt a chill. I didn't like the way the conversation was going but I didn't know how to stop her. Kate wanted to tell me about it.

"So he rented this plane," she said. "The damn fool. The damn fool. Slipped away during the reception and we were all wondering where he was. We were all out on the back lawn, right over there where you found Jane's body. A really beautiful day. And the next thing we saw, Harrison was up there, trailing smoke in the sky. He wrote HAPPY. In smoke. HAPPY. I told you he was from California. Then he started doing tricks, stalls and spins and loops. He looped it right into Clam Pond while we were all watching on Jane's lawn, his parents too. Broke his neck and drowned to boot. The Coast Guard came."

That was when MouMou gave it another try, walked

forward to the couch with great reserve and dignity, not about to beg. I was proud of that old dog, proud to be associated with her at that moment, but when I reached down to give her a pat of support she turned and snapped at me. This was her show.

"Okay, come on up here, sister, but no tricks," Kate said to her. She snapped her fingers and MouMou flew into her lap. "So, I'm thirty-one and I guess the nuns still have their hooks into me. Harrison knew where I was coming from. Sweet guy. Willing to wait. We had a Catholic wedding, mass, the works."

"You know what? I'm going to go out in the kitchen and try to find us something to eat."

"I'm not hungry. Really. I couldn't eat a bite."

"Neither of us had dinner, Kate."

She put her arm around my shoulder, friend to friend, confiding a great secret. "Don't you get it? Don't you understand? What you have here, what you actually have here is a virgin widow."

"I've got some English muffins I can toast, and peanut butter."

"Well? Don't you think that's funny?" Kate asked.

SEVEN

I HAD NO TELEPHONE IN THE house to call a wrecker at the one full-service station that was open in winter and there were no cabs. North Walpole's only cab company simply closed down from December through April. I guess I could have walked over to the cop on duty at the Drexel house and asked for help, but that idea didn't seem to occur to Kate, and I didn't suggest it because I wanted her to spend the night with me. I was lonely, pure and simple.

"McFarland, you've got to do something or you're going to have another corpse on your hands," she said. "I'm freezing to death."

The big fire I'd made had died down and the house was cold again. I got dressed in my winter gear and, still sore and aching, trooped outside to pry wood from the big frozen pile. The sleet had glistened the surface of the snow in the yard. It crunched under my boots as I walked to the woodpile and the sleet rattled on the surface of my shell parka. Cold and windy.

I made three trips, limping all the way, returning with big heavy armloads of water-soaked hardwood, and never saying one word to Kate Bingham who sat on the couch, long legs tucked under her, with MouMou lying contentedly in her lap, zonked out as she always was when she was exactly where she wanted to be.

On my first trip back with the wood Kate said, "I know all the things you're going to say to me. Frigid, uptight Catholic bitch. Blah, blah, blah. Right?" I looked at her without answering and left for the woodpile.

On my second trip back she said, "Well, I've heard all that before. And it's true, I admit it. So what have you got to say to that?" I still managed to keep my mouth shut.

Back from my last trip, I laid a stack of the wet wood on the hot coals and the wood went crazy, popping, hissing, steaming, before it burst into flame.

"You're old enough to be my father almost," Kate said. "Overweight, too. And I've got a hunch you're down on your luck in ways I don't even know about."

"You are correct on all counts. Will you have dinner with me tomorrow night? Somewhere nice, your choice."

She glared at me. "*Yes!* Because I'm bored."

"You're the best-looking woman I ever saw in my life."

"Jesus, you are a strike-out artist, McFarland."

I got one of the blankets off the cot and wrapped it around her shoulders. She didn't protest. "Have you got any Coke or anything like that?" she asked.

"My wife's name was Earline."

"How could anybody marry *anybody* with a name like that?"

"We're getting divorced."

"Give me a break, will you?"

"No kids. And I don't love her. Never did."

"I mean, *look*. You're probably a nice guy and all that, but this really is a little much for me to cope with."

"Then tell me to go to hell."

"Go to hell. No, I really didn't mean that."

"I'm not playing games."

98

"Well, I don't know about this."

"I'll feed you. For openers." A slumber-party snack, that's what it was. I found some Coke and I browned English muffins in the old toaster oven and spread peanut butter on them. We ate all four.

"Stay here with me?"

She nodded her head. Looked at me, all of a sudden the bluest eyes I ever saw. Or green, violet maybe. Somewhere in there. "Yes."

I joined the rolling daybed to the sofa and spread the blankets, and we took off our shoes and turned in. The sleet was bouncing off the roof and the wind was blowing but the fire was nice and warm now. I turned off the living-room lights.

We lay on our backs, side by side. "How the hell can you live like this?" she asked. "You're one step away from being a bum."

"To tell the truth, it's been a long time since I felt better. I'll get the furnace fixed tomorrow."

"I know a guy I'll send around."

"I've really needed somebody to take me under her wing."

"Up yours. What am I doing here? Please tell me that."

"Spending the night with me, I guess you'd call it."

"I will tell you something really astounding, McFarland. This is actually the first time in my entire life I've ever spent the entire night with a man, slept alongside him I mean. Not even with Harrison. Can you believe that, at my age?"

"It's like jungle warfare, Kate. One yard at a time."

"I don't even know you."

"You're lonely. You're sad. And you need a friend. Also, you're trapped."

"Are you sure you're not some closet creep? If you are I'll kill you."

I was gazing up at the ceiling, looking at the patterns the light from the fire was making. *Tell her.* "You'd be no safer in a convent, Kate. Earline left me all screwed up. Can't get it up these days. I'm telling you, babe, we're made for each other."

Silence, then a sigh. "Well, isn't this simply beautiful." I put my arm around her and she snuggled up to me. "You don't realize it but I am a very difficult person. I mean, I am very strong willed."

"Let's just try it and see. Please?"

She leaned over and kissed me, then placed her head on my chest. "We'll see. You are not what I had in mind at all. Put your other arm around me, McFarland. And hold me. I mean, I'm willing to give it a chance. I think."

We went to sleep that way, leaving it at that.

Funeral services for Jane Northrop Sexon Drexel were held the following Thursday morning at eleven o'clock at Saint Matthew's Episcopal Church, the Reverend Paul Rowley officiating. Kate and I overslept. You heard that right.

The moment I woke up I knew we were in trouble. It was much too light outside on such a winter's day. I looked at my watch and winced. Kate was sound asleep with the blankets pulled over her head, and MouMou was down under there with her somewhere.

I slipped out of bed without waking either of them and went into the kitchen where, I remembered, I had stashed away a big bottle of V-8 juice. I uncapped it, drank about half of it, refilled the bottle with vodka, shook it and took it in to Kate. "Wake up. Wake up and drink this. You got a tough day ahead of you."

She propped herself up on one elbow, never looked prettier, drank from the bottle I held out to her, and shuddered.

"It's really late, isn't it? I'm afraid to look at my watch."

"Don't look. We've got time. Are you in charge of arrangements?"

"No. Shouldn't you say you're glad I'm here or good morning, or something?"

"Good morning. I'm going to fall in love with you. And who's in charge of the arrangements?"

"Noah and the church and the funeral home. I took care of the flowers and picked out a dress for her. Do I have time to go home and dress? I've got a black wool dress I was going to wear."

"No, you don't. Kate, it's ten-thirty."

"Holy Jesus!"

After that it was blind flight, as I had known it would be. Kate jumped out of bed running. She had slept in her jeans and her sweater. She jammed her feet into her shoes, slipped into her down vest and ran in panic out the front door, shouting, "Come on!" I pulled on my shoes, threw on my old Burberry raincoat, grabbed the bottle, and followed her. By the time I got to her car she already had the engine started, but the wheels were spinning in reverse on the ice. Hopeless.

"Forget it!" I yelled. "Come on." We ran up the driveway, slipping and sliding, holding hands. The young police officer on morning duty in the Drexel driveway had a neat mustache and wore dark aviator's sunglasses even though the morning sky was dark. He was drinking coffee out of a Bob's Sandwich Shop cup. He rolled his car window down when we ran up, took off his glasses and smiled. A goofy-looking guy who had a gold tooth. "Joggers? Mighty cold for that."

"Officer, we need a ride to the church, please. To Mrs. Drexel's funeral."

"Wish I could oblige you."

"I don't know you," Kate said. "Are you a regular member of the force?"

"No. I'm a special. Department-store security guard over in Hyannis. But I'm a graduate of the Barnstable police training course. So Chief Simmons hires me as a temporary when he needs extra help."

"Chief Simmons is going to be very upset if you don't get this lady to Saint Matthew's on time for that funeral."

"Mister, I can't leave my post. I'm under strict orders."

"This is Mrs. Bingham, officer. Mrs. Harrison Bingham. The lady who's going to give all that money away."

"Why didn't you say so? Get in!"

We jumped in the backseat and off we roared, burning rubber. "Drink some of this," I told Kate, offering her the bottle. "Settle your stomach."

"Care to see the morning *Globe*, Mrs. Bingham?" the young madman in uniform asked, handing the paper back to us as he hit 60 MPH on an icy street. "Story's on the front page."

Indeed, it was. They had played it big, front page above the fold, with an old picture which was captioned *Jane Sexon Drexel, 1938 photograph*. No byline, of course. Special to the *Globe*.

"No wonder you were her pet," I said. "When she was in her early thirties she looked enough like you to be your sister."

"Boy, this thing has really put North Walpole on the map," the insane cop said as he roared through a stop sign, pedal to metal. "People are even talking about it in Hyannis."

Kate took the paper from my hands and examined the picture. "No, I don't see it."

"Well, I do. *You* can't see much of anything."

"I'd say this probably is the greatest day in this town's

whole history," the speed freak said, sliding around an icy curve. "Hell, I'm going to give you folks siren and flashing lights. Let 'em know we're coming."

I hit the bottle again and passed it to Kate. "Mac, we're going to be killed and I've just met you. Also, I am a mess," she moaned.

"Officer, you got a raincoat by any chance?"

"I could get one back at headquarters."

"Mrs. Bingham here needs one desperately."

"Hold on! You got it!" The maniac hit his brakes, did a 180 on the ice, wiggled the rear end of the car a bit, and roared off in the opposite direction. "I can't see a damn thing," he protested.

"It might help if you'd take off those shades."

"Right!" He pulled his sunglasses off and threw them in the empty seat beside him.

"Give me that bottle," Kate said.

"What's your name?" I asked the demented young temporary.

"They call me Lucky."

"Well, Lucky, Chief Simmons will certainly be made aware of the way you are performing your duties today."

"Hot stuff! Hold on!" Lucky did a slip-slide into the police headquarters parking lot and was out of the car, racing to the entrance before we had come to a final stop.

"What time is it?" Kate asked.

"We've got five minutes." We had two. "Look, they won't start without you. They'll give you a few minutes."

I had a small comb which I handed to her. Using the rearview mirror, she pulled the comb through her hair, muttering, "Oh, God, look at me," etc., then got a small makeup kit from the pocket of her vest and quickly worked on her lips, eyes and cheeks, dabbing, brushing, quickly drawing lines on her face.

Lucky came running out of the station waving a black nylon raincoat as if it were a Nazi flag he'd captured during the Battle of the Bulge. Kate got out of the car, put on the raincoat, pulled the belt tightly around her waist, rolled her jeans up above her knees, and suddenly looked like a million dollars.

Kate was one of those rare and fortunate women who never had to bother much about her looks, who lived secure in the knowledge that no matter how messy she looked, given a few moments to shake herself out, she became beautiful and elegant. Except for the L. L. Bean shoes and that couldn't be helped that morning.

"Let's go to church, Lucky, and don't spare the horses," I said. We were catapulted out of the parking lot.

"I picked Jane's burial dress," Kate said. "There was nobody else to do it. She always liked bright colors, especially as she grew older. So I chose a bright dress she loved. Wore it all the time in the summer. Maybe a black one would have been better."

"I'm sure it was a good choice."

"What do you know, McFarland? Jane's going to heaven dressed in a three-year-old yellow-linen Perry Ellis."

Lucky took us through the tight streets of North Walpole as if they were the tracks of a roller coaster, with top lights flashing, siren sounding and horn blowing. Truly in his natural element. Fortunately there were no orphans or widows crossing the streets. "Here we are, folks," he shouted as he pulled up to the entrance of the church. "And I sure hope you enjoyed the ride!"

There were three television camera crews and four or five reporters waiting on the sidewalk. My story had had an effect. Young men and women wearing heavy makeup and red and green blazers with breast pocket insignia—*Impact News!*—recognized Kate and tried to thrust microphones in her face when she got out of the patrol car.

She lunged forward, muttering, "Keep the hell away from me." She was a slightly pigeon-toed woman and even walking on a flat sidewalk she looked as if she were hiking the Appalachian Trail down hill, about to stumble forward, out of control. Also, I realized, the vodka had done its job only too well.

"Mrs. Bingham is most distraught," I told the gang. "She'll have nothing to say."

"Okay. But the fuzz has sealed off the graveyard," said an old-timer, which meant a guy about my age.

"I promise I'll get a full pool report to you," I said.

"Bloodsuckers," Kate hissed when I caught up with her in the vestibule of the church.

"Yes. And to think I used to do that full time for a living."

We went inside. "Well, would you just look at this," she whispered. "Would you look at this."

The people of North Walpole had turned out in force for Jane Drexel's funeral. No doubt the money she had left behind had something to do with it, that along with natural curiosity. But maybe some people had come because of all the things she already had done for their town. In any event, the church was filled to its capacity. Kate and I were seated in the front pew with Noah, Bascombe, Gerald Dickerson and a young couple I assumed was John Norton and his wife.

And we were right on time. Noah's policemen, all in full dress uniform, were serving as ushers. A brass quintet from the North Walpole town band, middle-aged men dressed in old, shiny red uniforms, was playing a medley of hymns. Members of the Colonial Color Guard were in place along both walls, standing at attention, and members of the volunteer fire department, whose grand new pump truck she had purchased, served as pallbearers. The entire board of selectmen occupied the second pew. It was a tribute, nothing less.

The young Reverend Mr. Rowley nervously read from the Book of Common Prayer. "We brought nothing into this world, and it is certain we can carry nothing out."

But you can leave things behind, and Jane Drexel certainly had done that. She had left a lot of money and a big mess.

The graveside service was private. Noah had seen to that by stationing police officers at the entrance and at every corner of the old wrought-iron fence that surrounded the graveyard, and he'd had the good sense to rope off a small area on a rise outside the fence as a press compound. The television crews had mounted their cameras there on tripods, with long-range lenses and a clear view. They had no complaints.

"Unto Almighty God we commend the soul of our sister departed, and we commit her body to the ground," the Reverend Mr. Rowley intoned.

With special permission obtained from the town's board of selectmen—and God knows who else—the old lady's body was being buried in a far corner of North Walpole's historic Colonial graveyard, whose ancient tilted and blackened stones bore carvings of grinning angels of death and dim inscriptions, words chiseled so long ago that they could not be made out anymore.

"The Lord be with you."

"And with thy spirit," the nine of us replied more or less in unison.

One of them, I thought. It had to be one of them.

Noah Simmons, his tiny wife Dede beside him, about half his size, wore his full dress uniform with polished brass buttons on his overcoat, gold scrambled eggs on the brim of his cap, and a golden eagle on each shoulder. The Chief. Many of Noah's ancestors surely lay moldering under those old gray stones. *She put me through college. Paid for every cent of it.*

Bascombe Midgeley was dressed to attend the funeral of King George VI, homburg, chesterfield, black mourning band and three miniature medals affixed to the breast of the overcoat which attested to the fact that he had spent two years at sea aboard a Navy destroyer, including a six-month cruise with the U.S. Sixth Fleet in the Med. His wife was not there. *Yes, I grew up poor. . .*

Everything Gerald Dickerson wore was frayed, the cuffs of his trousers, coat cuffs, frayed tie knot, frayed shirt collar. His old herringbone overcoat was at least two sizes too small for him and I wondered which graduating shorto at Saint Tim's had left it behind hanging in a closet. He had a red rosebud pinned to his lapel. *Jane gave me money. From time to time. Over the years.*

"O God, whose mercies cannot be numbered; Accept our prayers on behalf of the soul of our servant departed." The minister sounded as if he wanted desperately to sneeze.

We all stood under a small tan awning which had been pitched over a carpet of green synthetic turf. The funeral home had provided no chairs. The sky above was flannel gray, threatening more sleet or snow or something any moment. Cold and windy as usual. Kate had rolled down the legs of her jeans.

She stood between me and John Norton, who turned out to be a tall, extremely handsome young man. He had one arm around his wife's shoulders and his other around Kate's and she appeared to be comfortable within the embrace; she had her arm around his waist.

Okay. Most people I know usually want one special person, an old friend, an old lover, to hold on to when they are sad or frightened and when big trouble comes if that special person is present they cleave to him, cannot help themselves. Kate had John Norton. Okay.

"Through Jesus Christ, to whom be glory for ever and ever, Amen. The service is over," the preacher said.

Gerald Dickerson unpinned the rosebud, knelt beside the grave and placed the flower on the lid of the casket. "I shall come and visit you frequently, I promise, dear Jane," he said softly. The old man stayed on his knees while the rest of us moved slowly away from the graveside.

Kate, speaking in a whisper, introduced me to John Norton and his wife, Sarah. "The Nortons have invited us to lunch," she told me.

"Yes, all of you," John Norton said. "Noah? Bascombe?"

"Nothing fancy," his wife said. "I've made some vegetable soup." She had a rather long, horsey face, a lantern jaw, and a very warm, engaging smile. She looked like the sort of person you want on a committee.

"I guarantee it is good soup," her husband said.

Noah and Bascombe declined. Bascombe's wife was in bed with the flu and Noah said he had work to do.

"Well, we accept, don't we, Mac?" Kate said.

"Certainly. If I could use your phone for a few minutes."

"You working?" Noah asked. When he saw me walk inside the church with Kate a look of initial surprise and mild annoyance had shown on his face until I gave him a look which tried to say "Only trying to help out," and he had nodded in reply, "Okay, I understand."

"Well, yes," I said to him. "You see all those cameras? Hell, they're zooming in, taking pictures of all of you while we stand here talking. It's a big story, Noah, and I can't help that."

"Any progress?" Bascombe asked. "Any breakthrough yet?"

"Nothing I can talk about. But we're getting there."

"Can I use that? And quote you?" I asked.

"Why not."

"Listen, people, we've got to hold a meeting of the board of trustees pretty soon," John Norton said. "We can use the boardroom at the bank, if you like."

"Fine with me. Sometime next week maybe," Kate said.

"We have a lot of things to get settled. Election of officers, for example."

"Let's give poor old Jane a chance to get settled in her grave," Noah said. "We're not in that much of a hurry, are we?"

"I'll give all of you fair warning. I'm going to insist that all the dividends be deposited at Pilgrim," John Norton said. "Let's keep it at home. No need to use some bank in Boston or New York."

"I see nothing inherently wrong with that," Bascombe said.

Mr. Dickerson had joined us. "There is also the matter of fees and expenses," he said. "I assume all of us will be paid a fee to serve on the board. It's customary. Am I correct?"

"We'll get *around* to all that," Kate protested.

"And there is the question of what to do about the property. Including my old wreck of a summer cottage. I assume, as a board member, I'll be allowed to keep it."

"I've got some very definite ideas about investments," John Norton said.

"It seems to me we're holding our first board meeting right here and now," Noah said.

"Yes, and I am freezing to death," Kate said.

"Oh, we certainly can't go into such things now," Norton said. "But if we use that money wisely we can do a lot for our little town."

"I must warn you that there still remains a considerable amount of legal work to set this whole thing in motion," Bascombe said.

"Why not meet at Jane's house next week? Could we do that, Noah?"

"I'm afraid not, Kate. We've got to keep that house locked and sealed for the time being."

"I was thinking we could turn the house into preservation society headquarters and run the trust from there. Have offices."

"A very good idea. Just don't count on it being available anytime soon."

Bascombe glanced at me in regal disapproval. "Mc-Farland, after all, my good fellow. Exactly what are you doing here? A common journalist. A snoop. And this is private business. I must protest." Half joking but half serious, he was making a point.

"Mac's with me and that's that," Kate said immediately, looking around, daring any of them to challenge her.

"As far as I'm concerned this is all off the record," I said. "Not a word of it will get in the paper. Scout's honor. Except I did promise to file a pool report to the others on the graveside service. I'll do that on the way to the Nortons'."

"I guess we are having our first board meeting in a way," Kate said. "Johnny, how much money is in Jane's account at the bank?"

"Had she written any big checks lately, to your knowledge, Katey?"

"No."

Norton thought for a moment. "Then I'd say around two million. That's about the level she usually kept it at. Our largest, needless to say."

"I ask because we *are* going to need some cash right away. Bascombe will have expenses and so will I," Kate told him.

"Jane's will directs that her husband's body be removed from Boston and reburied beside her here," Bascombe said. "That's what?, a couple of thousand probably right there. It's also going to cost a considerable amount to close her house in Florida and pay off the servants there."

"No problem your friendly hometown banker can't solve," Johnny Norton said. "What do you need? Twenty, thirty thousand? I'll just make a temporary bridge loan to the trust. We can get that taken care of first thing tomorrow. Even this afternoon if you like."

"Mr. Arithmetic," Noah said with a smile.

John Norton put his arm around Kate's waist and gave her a squeeze. "That's me. That's what you guys used to call me, wasn't it?"

"They called you that because you were so very, very bright at math, John," Mr. Dickerson said. "Of the four of you, you were quite the best at figures." He paused. "I suppose this really isn't the proper time or place to get into the matter of fees, is it?" He looked quite despondent.

John Norton turned his head and gave the rest of us a quick wink. He was a good-looking guy, no question about that, as handsome as a model in a Ralph Lauren ad. He was wearing a navy blue cashmere overcoat, collar turned up, with a lighter blue scarf around his neck. About Kate's age, damn him.

"You do have a special problem," he said to the old man. "With this trust you've got all sorts of new responsibilities you hadn't counted on. And you're living on a retirement income, after all, and the rest of us aren't."

"That is correct, John."

"So I'll just make the loan to the trust for thirty-five thousand. And I'll make out a five-thousand-dollar cashier's check for you. You can pick it up tomorrow morning, Mr. Dickerson. Is that okay with everybody?"

"That is most generous of you, my boy."

"Hey, it's not my money. The bank will draw interest on the loan to the trust. Which has a *lot* of money." He looked around. "Do we all agree?"

There was no dissent. By unspoken agreement, the members of the North Walpole trust seemed to have decided that its very first endowment would be used to supplement the meager retirement income of their old summer-school teacher.

"How very, very nice of you all," he murmured. "Could we make it ten?"

"Why not?" Noah said. "I vote yes."

"Mille gratiae, studens bonus meus."

"Satis pecuniae est, magister venerabilis."

"Noah was every bit as good at language as John was at math."

"Okay, okay, but let's not make a habit out of this," Kate said. "Jane didn't leave that money for us to spend on ourselves." She looked around the cemetery. "My mother missed the funeral."

"Oh, Kate, with everything else going on, I forgot to tell you," Noah said. "There was yet another head-on out on Route Six. She called me and said to tell you she's working in the emergency room and couldn't make it."

Taps? A man dressed in a red uniform was standing at the gate of the old graveyard with a trumpet at his lips. The television cameras had all focused on him, of course.

"They wanted to do it and I didn't have the heart to refuse them," Noah said. "Jane had bought the band new lightweight uniforms for the concerts next summer. The old ones they'd been wearing were a disgrace. It's their way of saying thanks."

Snow as light and airy as old plaster dust began to fall. The Colonial graveyard was on a round hill which looked over the town, a town of gray shingles and snow-covered roofs, its boundaries defined by the gray salt ponds, with yellow light the color of old ivory shining from the windows of its houses. North Walpole on Cape Cod.

I looked at the five of them as they stood there while the town bugler played. Gerald Dickerson bowed his head. Kate wiped away a tear. Noah saluted. Bascombe placed his homburg over his heart. And Norton had his arm around Kate.

One of them . . . , I thought. I would have bet money on it.

EIGHT

SARAH NORTON'S BEEF VEG-
etable soup did indeed prove to be delicious, perfect fare
for a raw Cape Cod winter afternoon. With it she served
hot cornbread and unsalted butter. Kate and I pigged out.

The Nortons lived in a comfortable home, filled with
good, traditional furniture, and with a water view of Pilgrim Harbor. A nice house but no mansion. Through the
dining-room window I could see whitecaps on the water,
which meant at least twenty knots of wind. It was still snow-
ing.

There were only the four of us and we chatted as we ate.
Sarah said so much snow was unusual on the Cape because
the Gulf Stream's proximity helps moderate the winters.
And, her husband added, that is one reason more and more
retired people were settling here as year-round residents.
One coat cooler than Boston in summer, one coat warmer
in winter. We didn't talk about the funeral.

I praised the soup. "Maui onions," he said. "We brought
some back when we were there. For Christmas."

"I'm sure your postcard will arrive any day now," Kate
said.

Sarah announced she had baked an apple pie, and left
for the kitchen to get it.

"We adopted another kid while we were out there," John Norton told Kate.

"How many does that make? A couple of dozen?"

"Six. This is a Cambodian child. She's in an orphanage in Kahoolawe. Sad tale. Her parents got out, he was a professional man, and they made it all the way to the islands, then both of them were killed in a traffic accident. A three-year-old girl." He turned to me. "Sarah and I can't have children of our own."

"So they're gradually signing up to send the monthly support payments to half the orphans in the world."

"Oh, Kate. It isn't that much money. And it makes us both feel good."

Sarah had brought in the apple pie and was dishing it out. "If it tastes half as good as it looks and smells you ought to enter it in next fall's state fair," I told her and meant it. I tasted it. "I eat in awe."

"Now you see how she stole me away from Kate," Norton said. "It was her cooking. Sex had nothing to do with it."

"They were teenage sweethearts," Sarah said to me, smiling, with absolutely no hint of jealousy in her voice. "For one torrid summer."

"During that summer school?" I asked.

"Exactly. Then Kate went off to Wellesley and I left for New Haven," Norton said.

"And one month later, on a blind date, he met Sarah and I never heard from him again, except for an occasional Christmas card." Kate smiled at Sarah affectionately. They were obviously close friends.

A phone rang. I hadn't noticed but there was a telephone in their dining room, discreetly positioned, a dark brown phone which sat on an elegant burl walnut console within reach of Norton's right hand. "Hello?" he said. "Can I sell you some money today?"

"He's on the phone all the damn time, morning, noon and night," Sarah said, not unhappily. "I finally gave up and had extensions put in every room of the house, even the bathrooms."

"Okay! Olé, José!" John shouted into the phone. "Tell him we'll give him the loan, sixty, ten years, at our current rate. Provided." He winked at Kate. "Provided that the North Walpole Preservation Society gets to approve the exterior design. Okay?"

"Johnny, what is this? What are we approving?"

"Italian kid. Hardworking kid, nice kid. Eight years' experience working in a Pizza Hut in Hyannis, assistant manager. He wants to build a new place of his own just down from the commercial fishing pier in South Walpole. Pizzas and fried clams. You heard what I said about it."

The phone rang again. "Hello?"

"See?" Sarah said.

"Mrs. Adams, what can I say? I have read and very carefully considered your loan application. My wife, Sarah, has been buying your jams and jellies for years at the arts and crafts fair every summer. Mrs. Adams, you are talking to a personal fan of yours when you are talking to me. I read your loan application and I asked myself, if I approve this loan, will it mean Mrs. Adams will go commercial on me and I'll have no more of her wild beach plum jelly to spread on my toast every morning?"

"It really is good," Sarah said to us.

"And then I thought, provided she keeps that homemade taste, what sort of person am I to deprive the rest of mankind of the pleasure of Mrs. Adams's jams and jellies? So here's the deal. The loan is yours. Provided that you guarantee to supply me one dozen jars of wild beach plum jelly every year. Okay?" He smiled and enjoyed listening for a moment to Mrs. Adams's screams of joy. "Quiet down now.

Come in tomorrow and we'll give you the money." He hung up the phone, shrugged his shoulders and smiled at us. "I guess I'm financing a jam and jelly shop."

I liked John Norton immensely at that moment. I decided he was a good and decent man. Evil usually is easy to spot but the quality of genuine goodness often is difficult to recognize. John you couldn't help but like the minute you met him.

He was enthusiastic and ebullient, friendly and outgoing, with a ready smile, a person obviously anxious to please, to accommodate; a bit of a bullshitter maybe, but so charming and well mannered that he really didn't know or care about how handsome and elegant he was, a child of wonder, a Golden Boy who had known the exact moment to leave the beach behind and grow up. He also appeared to be both hardworking and civic-minded, concerned about and committed to the right things; a booster who didn't let it get out of hand. No wonder Kate was drawn to him and thought of him as someone special. He *was* someone special. Even his wife seemed to like him.

"Do I get to approve the exterior of the new jam and jelly shop, Johnny?" Kate asked him.

"Why not? The longest journey begins with a single step, they say." He was pouring cognac from a handsome crystal decanter while Sarah poured coffee. "If we use that trust money wisely we can make a difference here, Kate."

We finished the pie and Sarah led us into the living room. She had a fire going. Very cozy.

"I've been thinking about it a lot," Kate said, settling into an armchair. "I don't think we should rush headlong into anything, Johnny. That's the most important thing. We've got to sit down and decide among ourselves what the mission of the trust should be."

"It seems to me Jane pretty much spelled that out in her

will. Preservation, beautification, cultural and social enhancement of life. Isn't that how it reads?"

"Which can be interpreted by us any number of ways. I don't think we should go galloping off in all directions, is what I'm saying. We need a focus, maybe even bylaws, a charter. From the very beginning."

"I certainly have no argument with that."

"I've even thought that maybe we ought to invite some outside experts to offer their views."

"Sure, and have every old lady on the Cape telling us to spend every cent of the money buying up land to prevent overdevelopment."

"I'm convinced that control of future growth should be our principal mission. You know how Jane was on the subject. And it *is* her money."

"Growth and change are inevitable here, Kate."

"May I ask a question?" I said. "As an out-of-towner? Everybody here seems so concerned about development. But I ride around and I don't see any instant slums being thrown up all over the place. I see pretty nice construction is what I see."

"That's not a question, that's a statement," Kate said.

"You know what I'm aiming at."

"Mac, the problem is that it's just so nice here," Sarah said. "The Cape has a limited amount of land and, it seems, a limitless number of people who want to build on it. We're going through growth shock."

"Did you know there was more new home construction in the town of Barnstable last year than there was in the city of Boston?" Kate said. "Half-acre lots going for thirty, forty thousand dollars, land is so scarce. In a few years working people won't be able to afford to live here."

"Growth here has been nothing short of fantastic," John said. "And it's just beginning. I've seen projections showing a seventy percent additional population increase during the next fifteen years."

"No way to control it?" I asked.

"Oh, some places have tried," Kate said. "They've tried building moratoriums, building-permit limits, open space plans. And nothing seems to work. We are becoming a suburb of Boston."

"I think if we used the trust money wisely we could make some difference here in North Walpole," John said. "Maybe not much, but some."

"What would you do?" Kate asked.

"What we're going to do with Mrs. Adams's jam shop. Take your average developer. He's put together, say, forty acres of land, surveyed it, cleared it."

"And named it *North Cape Condo Heaven*," Kate said.

"No. *Cape Life!* With an exclamation point," Sarah said.

"Even better. Perfect. The exclamation point was his wife Irene's idea." Kate clapped her hands in approval.

"Wait now," John said. "There are good developers and bad developers here, and believe me I know these guys. This is a nice guy, college graduate, intends to build quality housing and hopes to make a decent profit. Is he committing any crime?"

"Yes. Rape!" Kate cried. "Rape of the Cape."

"Kate, you're swimming against the tide. The current is against you."

"Johnny, Johnny, the whole place is going to *sink*."

"My point is, the developer's got the land but he needs money to build. So we'll loan him the money. Provided he agrees to meet our specs as to lot size, land use, maybe even design approval. And I'm saying that's what some of the trust money should be used for."

"Well, it sounds like a good idea, I guess." Kate frowned. "I just wonder if that's what Jane would have wanted."

"She wasn't very specific, was she? It seems to me that she worded the will to give us broad discretionary powers."

"I'm sure of only one thing. Jane very definitely wanted to buy the Hollings property and I think we ought to go ahead with that."

"Sorry. I don't agree, Kate," he said immediately.

"I wish you'd explain."

"We don't have unlimited funds, not nearly enough to buy every piece of waterfront property around here. We're going to have to pick and choose. And much of the land we want may well be priced out of our range."

"You have a point there," she said.

"I've been meaning to ask you. Did Jane give you any advance notice about the trust she was creating?"

"Not a word, not a clue."

"Nor me. And I would have loved to have had a role in setting it up. Bascombe might have said *something*. I *am* a banker, after all."

"Bascombe was pledged to secrecy by Jane, Johnny, and you know how strict he is about that lawyer-client business. Besides, Jane hadn't exactly planned on dying so soon. Less than a week after she signed her new will. She expected to be around for years, and if she had been I'm sure we all would have been told about the trust and would have been allowed to help structure it into its final form. As it is, we're stuck with what we've got."

"Kate's right, Johnny," Sarah said. "Johnny thinks that with anything involving money he should be there with his calculator."

Kate sighed. "What a mess. We still have Jane's entire, rather complicated life left to sort out."

"At least Bascombe's the executor and not some group of Wall Street strangers."

I finished the last of my cognac. "And in case it's skipped

your minds, there is still a little matter of an unsolved murder."

"You know what I think?" John Norton said. "I don't think they'll ever find out who killed her."

"Somebody hopes you're right," I said.

NINE

KATE BECAME TEMPORARILY famous. How could she not have? The beautiful young woman who had all that money to give away. A natural, the sort of story any competent news editor would immediately pull out of the stack of morning wire copy and mark for inclusion in that day's edition.

I wrote a long story about her for the *Globe*. She begged me not to but I did it anyway. I know a good newspaper story when I see one and it has been my experience that somebody else from across the street will write it if you don't, which causes editors to use bad language, throw glue pots and bite through cigars.

A week passed. *The New York Times* sent a reporter to write a piece similar to mine. The *Today* show sent a correspondent and a camera crew to do a spot on the little town that had struck it rich. *Good Morning, America* wanted to fly Kate to New York by chartered plane for a live interview, but she turned them down. *People* sent a photographer who took her picture with the town behind her. It was a full-court media press.

Kate handled it all very well. Most people don't, but fleeting fame didn't seem to matter to her. She seemed to understand it for what it was, a quick kiss in the kitchen during a party, pleasant enough perhaps but signifying nothing.

She also quietly but firmly took charge of my personal life, which pleased me no end. She knew how to get things done and who could do them, knew everybody in town by first name. When she walked down Main Street people in cars honked and waved at her.

Somebody, I don't know who, came and repaired the floor furnace, and thank God for that because North Walpole was experiencing its worst winter in years. The wind howled through the town. The red warning flag flew constantly at the Coast Guard station. A fishing boat sank in a gale. A real bitch of a winter, everybody at Bob's said.

Another repairman came, took a look at the old coil-top refrigerator and laughed until tears welled in his eyes. He even called his partner and told him for Christ sake he ought to come take a look at this thing. But he got it running again and I no longer had to use the front steps as a freezer. He also repaired the old electric stove and installed a space heater he found in the garage, which warmed things up considerably in the kitchen.

I got a telephone. A laundry man knocked on the door and took all my dirty clothes away. A big, red-faced cleaning woman appeared one morning, announced that Katherine Mary had sent her, took a long look at the living room and whispered "Jeeeesus!" But when she left the place was clean for the first time since I had moved in. Even the windows.

I tell you, all I needed to make the scene complete was an ascot, a red smoking jacket, a pair of velvet slippers and a pipe.

Kate would have made a great amphibious-assault beach master. It was in her nature to keep things moving. She made decisions quickly and acted on them without misgiving or second thought. Given authority, she went right to work and kept on doing things as she saw fit until somebody stopped her—and this time there was nobody to do that.

Using the money from the bridge loan John Norton arranged, she rented an office suite in the Commercial Building, filled it with office furniture which she leased from a firm in Hyannis, had phones installed, ordered new stationery, and hired a temporary secretary named Bridget. All in the space of a few days. Kate didn't mess around.

Good thing, too, because during that week the requests for money came pouring in. It was amazing the number of worthwhile causes and endeavors the good people of North Walpole came up with, once it became known that money might be available to pay for them.

A retired history professor wanted to research and write a definitive history of the town. A three-year project. Something in the neighborhood of a fifty-thousand-dollar grant would do the trick.

A landscape gardener wanted a contract to build a new stone wall around the Colonial cemetery—a proposal Kate thought had merit. The Boy Scouts wanted a new meeting lodge and the Sea Scouts wanted a new Boston whaler. A builder wanted to restore the old train depot and turn it into a museum. The minister of the Congregational church wanted a new office addition and the Catholic priest wanted a new heating plant for the parish school.

A new summer theater. Money to clear away the silver-maple trees which obscured the view of the inlets and money to plant more lilies along the banks. Money to build a new, better-lighted gazebo in the park for the Friday night summer band concerts, to launch a classical-music festival, to increase the number of books in the town library.

There was no lack of ideas and suggestions on how to spend that money and, truly, the annual income from the trust would be so huge that none of them was entirely unfeasible. The problem was that there was no money available for anything just yet and, at Kate's frantic request, I reported this fact in the *Globe*.

Noah Simmons seemed to be making no progress in his investigation of Jane Drexel's murder or, if he was, he wasn't talking about it. The week passed without anything new about the murder for me to write about. Dave Farkas kept me on full salary but I was holding my breath.

Kate was living with me, more or less. She was still living at her mother's house, for the record, but she had a separate entrance, a separate small apartment, really; her mother worked goofy hours at the hospital in Hyannis, and Kate came and went as she pleased.

She was a pleasant and considerate part-time roommate who never left the bathroom messy and who did her share. She bought a small black-and-white television set at the hardware store so we could sit together on the couch before the fire and watch the late-night movies. She turned out to be a pretty good cook, nothing fancy. Most of all she was good company.

There was a small downstairs bedroom and bath off the living room and I invested part of my first week's salary in a new electric heater. We slept there, all bundled up, with her in my arms. A pleasure. But, God damn Earline, I was still out of commission, not that it mattered. After all, I still had a very determined thirty-one-year-old chaste Catholic on my hands. We hugged and kissed a lot, though.

"I'm not frigid," she told me one of those nights when we were in bed together. "And I am not a dyke. Men excite me sexually, not women, in any way. I'm not sexually uptight, either. The idea of sex doesn't scare me."

"What the hell are you then?"

"I'm Catholic, damn you. Can't you understand?"

"What do you think would happen if you just said to hell with it?"

"Do you mean, do I believe God would kill me with a thunderbolt if I spread my legs right now and allowed you to penetrate me?"

"I guess . . . something like that."

"No, I don't. It's just that I had it drilled into me by the Church that this is the only truly moral way for a woman to live her life."

"What do they know about fucking in Vatican City?"

"Not much. I agree. And a lot of Catholic women, women I know, just ignore the Church when it comes to that. And I would, too, when it comes to birth control."

"But not sexual intercourse."

"I know I sound like a little Irish teenager on an R.C. weekend retreat. I feel like one, too. But there you are."

"You don't feel like one." She was wearing a soft, pink flannel nightgown. "What do you want, Kate? Ask and I will do my damnedest to give."

"I want you to court me."

"I'm trying, I'm trying. I've got you in the sack with me, haven't I? That's progress in my book."

She gave me a punch in my ribs, a love lick not meant to hurt, but it did a little. "*Listen* to me. Court me and marry me. I love you. I don't give a damn that you're not Catholic. Or that you're getting divorced. I really don't care how many times you might have been married. Court me. I wanted to be courted. And marry me and I swear to God I'll give it to you morning, noon and night for the rest of my life. That's the way I want it, the way I've always wanted it, and I'm too damned old and you know I'm too damned stubborn to change my ways."

"I know that. I'll take you just the way you are."

"I'm your last and your best shot, too, Mac."

I didn't answer her because I knew she was right. Not one hundred percent. Maybe not my last shot but certainly my best.

"Well, I *am*," she said. "You're much too old for me. You're down on your luck. And I'm good-looking. I know I am because too many people have told me so."

"I hate to inform you of this, really I do, but the fact is *you're* almost too old for *me*, Kate."

"That's a laugh."

"The ancient Chinese believed a man should be with a woman half his age plus seven. I'm fifty, you're thirty-one. Add it up. You're right on the line, Kate, on the edge."

"That is the most stupid thing I ever heard."

"Also, you're blind as a bat, and you look like you're falling down a flight of stairs when you walk across a room."

"I do not!" Why do truly beautiful women like to hear things like that?

"You're pigeon-toed, Kate. Slightly pigeon-toed. Besides, there's always Mary Beth at the Binnacle."

"I would kill you. With my bare hands," she said. "I would murder you in your sleep."

So I courted Kate Bingham, the first time I ever had *courted* any woman. Earline and I had leapt into bed together before we knew much about each other. Two divers going off the cliff in Acapulco; one, two, three, *jump*. I wooed Kate, and another week passed. Still on salary, I was beginning to think the *Globe* had forgotten about me.

When she slept with me, which was almost every night that wicked winter, I always got up first and made the coffee, added half-and-half, and brought it to her to drink in bed while she woke up. Went out and started her car and turned on the heater so it would be nice and warm on her drive to work.

I drove her down to Hyannis for a Tex-Mex dinner at Sam Diego's and told her, "Heat up, bebe, because news-babering ha' been berry berry good to me. Muy rico." Silly shit like that.

I took her to the movies where we ate popcorn and watched wild-eyed child actors behaving as if they were scared half to death by the monstrous special-effects creations.

"I don't need this," I told her. "Life itself holds more than enough terror for me. I don't need any help from the kids from the UCLA film department."

"Shut up. Don't be such an old fogy." Her response.

One bright Saturday morning we walked Nauset beach with Noah, searching for interesting driftwood, a unique piece for him to use as a lamp base. An intense blue sky was dappled with puffy gray and white clouds and the big, coiled winter rollers crashing in filled our lungs with ice-cold ocean spray. We failed to find a suitable lamp base. We built a driftwood fire. Noah had a Thermos of black coffee and I produced a flask of Louis Roche calvados. We walked down the beach, Kate in the middle, with our arms around each other.

I cooked for her. I'm not much of a cook, not food-crazy, but as a bachelor for years I had cooked for myself and when the occasion demands it I'm up to it. Provided I have a detailed recipe, which I got at the public library.

"It is absolutely *de*vine!" she cried.

"Merely adequate, I'm afraid."

"It is just the best fish I have ever eaten in my entire life, that's all. Where'd you learn to make it?"

"By trial and error. It's my own creation."

A lover's lie. Page 263 of Craig Claiborne's *New York Times* cookbook. Fillets Plaza Athenée. You can look it up.

We went to the Binnacle, sat at the bar and watched the

Celtics games on Nickey's big color television set while we ate hamburgers and drank draft beer drawn for us by the voluptuous Mary Beth.

"The lettering on that window I helped pay for says SEAFOOD," I said to Nickey. "So where's the seafood?"

"It's coming. Expanded menu starting next summer."

"Bullcock," said Mary Beth. "Nickey is just full of bull-cock."

"It's bull*shit*!" Kate screamed at her.

Unrelenting pursuit, gentle persuasion, constant attention to detail, that was my formula. You ask, did it work? Are you kidding? You bet it did. Soon Kate began using salutations of endearment when she addressed me. "Hi, angel, I'm on my way," she would say on the phone when she called. "Honey bear, I cannot eat another bite." And when we got back to the house from that evening at the Binnacle, "Baby, I had such a good time tonight." I ate it up. What guy my age wouldn't? Especially coming from a woman such as she.

She ran the white flag up on a Sunday morning, a day I will never forget. We had stayed up late the night before watching *The Awful Truth* on television and we overslept. At ten o'clock Kate shook me awake and said, "Up. I'm having an attack. You got to get me to Bob's."

We dressed in winter gear, drove to Bob's Sandwich Shop and had breakfast—orange juice, coffee, pancakes and bacon for both of us—sitting at the counter, sharing a copy of the *Cape Cod Times*. Not a bad paper. Besides, all of the copies of the *Globe* were gone.

Bob's was, well, Bob's, the usual crowd. They all said hello to Kate and nodded at me. Warm and friendly, local banter, comments being passed back and forth about news stories. I was reading David Broder's column on the editorial page and Kate was reading the local news section when, without looking up from the paper, she quietly said, "Okay. This does it."

"Does what?" Broder was writing about the federal deficit. He thought it was way too big. I thought Kate hadn't found the pancakes to her taste.

"I just realized it sitting here. Jesus. Pancakes and the Sunday paper with you at the counter at Bob's. Not much."

"Want some more coffee?"

"Don't you understand what I'm telling you? You blockhead."

I folded the paper and put it on the counter. "No. Tell me, Kate." I thought I knew but I wanted to be sure.

"Well, it just came over me. It's what I want. If you want me."

"You got to be kidding. You serious, Kate?"

"I tell you I want to get laid and you ask me if I'm kidding?"

On the way home she reached over and touched me. For the first time. "My, you're all well," she said.

"I'm so excited I think I'm going to faint."

"Well, hurry. We'll see Father Riley tomorrow. One day more or less doesn't matter to me."

"Kate, my divorce isn't final. I don't know when it will be."

"Maybe they can back-date it or something like that. I really don't care. Just hurry."

I was driving a Buick I had rented from Hertz, as Dave Farkas had told me to do. I hadn't felt like this since before that afternoon I discovered and read Earline's infamous red diary. I took a corner too fast, slid on a patch of ice and glanced off a stone wall, scraping the right rear fender.

"Don't worry about it, darling. The insurance will pay for it," Kate said. "Just keep going. Get us home."

You should have seen that woman at that moment. Her

face was flushed, as red as a beet, her neck too, and she was wild-eyed and breathing quickly and deeply in her excitement. She looked like she was coming down with a case of the measles. Kate had come to a decision, a major crossroads in her life. Whoever would have thought that pancakes and the Sunday paper would have set her off?

"You okay?" I asked her, foolish question.

"Nervous as hell. You're going to have to lay down some guidelines, that's all."

"We'll take it easy. Don't worry."

"Just hurry home."

Except that Noah Simmons was waiting for us when we got to the house, blocking the entrance to the driveway with his Ford Fairlane police special. It was bad news, obviously. His face was grim.

"Come on. Get in," he said to us.

TEN

"**M**Y MOM'S DEAD, ISN'T SHE, Noah?" Kate said. "I know she is. You don't have to lie."

"Kate, I honestly don't know. All I know is what I've already told you came over the radio at headquarters. There's been an auto accident on Route Six and your mom's involved in it. It may amount to little or nothing."

"Oh, God." She put her face in her hands. "I just know she is." I put my arm around her.

"Kate's mother is a nurse in the emergency room at Cape Cod Hospital," Noah said. "On her way to work. Am I right, Katey?"

"Yes. She draws the Sunday afternoon shift about once a month. Please drive faster, Noah."

The local people call it Suicide Alley, and with good reason. A few miles east of Hyannis, Route 6, the principal mid-Cape highway, suddenly becomes a two-lane, two-way road. There are warning signs but occasionally a driver heading east from Hyannis forgets he is no longer on a four-lane divided highway, pulls out to pass slow-moving traffic at the crest of a hill and is met head-on by a car going in the opposite direction.

The Sunday traffic on the road heading west toward Hyannis was backed up all the way to the Chatham-Brewster exit, but Noah drove down the narrow grass border,

lights flashing and siren screaming. The traffic jam obviously was a bad omen, the sign of a big wreck and not
some fender bender, but neither Noah nor I said anything
about that.

"I'm glad you came and got me, Noah. Thank you," Kate
said.

"Yeah, well, I figured you'd want to go to her. *I* would
have. You weren't home so I went to Mac's. You two weren't
there but your car was, so I sat in the driveway and waited.
I wasn't there five minutes."

"Well, thanks. But she's dead. I know she is."

"Kate, we don't know anything yet."

"I'm telling you, my mom is dead, Mac."

Christ, what could I say? She was shivering with fear and
fright and trying to prepare herself for the worst. I could
only hold her, which I did. Also I prayed a little. *Please,
God, neither of us needs this.* Really dig into them, peel away
the layers, and most prayers ultimately are selfish, aren't
they?

It took us a half hour to get to the scene of the accident
and I wished it had taken longer, twice as long, forever,
because it was horrible, just a bloody mess. Two cars that
looked like two smashed bugs, metal intertwined, with glass
and oil everywhere, and with a gathering of state-police
cars, ambulances, wreckers and fire trucks. In his anxiety,
Noah drove up too close.

Kate screamed. "My mom's car! Look! I told you she's
dead, Mac. Didn't I tell you that?" She collapsed in my
arms, weeping and moaning. I held her tightly.

"Holy God," Noah said. "Mac, keep her here with you.
I'll check it out." He jumped out of the car and ran.

"I want to come!" Kate screamed. "I want to see my
mother!" She struggled in my arms but I managed to hold
on to her.

"Hold on, Kate. Noah will be right back. He wants us to wait right here. You heard him." She buried her face in my shoulder and wept. Kate knew. How could she not know? As a kid reporter, number two on the police beat, I covered my share of auto accidents and I'm telling you the Bionic Man dressed in a suit of stainless steel for extra protection could not have survived that wreck. No way.

So I held Kate and watched while Noah talked for two or three minutes with a group of state cops who kept pointing in all directions as they explained what happened. Satisfied, he walked slowly back to the car, shaking his head at me. *No.* I tightened my grip on Kate's shoulder. What good are prayers after the fact? It already had happened while I was praying for it not to have happened. I would remember that next time.

Noah brought with him a man who wore the black suit and the clerical collar of a priest, a guy who had a couple of things in common with me. He was about my age and he needed to lose a little weight. He got in the car, taking Noah's place behind the wheel. Noah got in the back. There was a pause, the way rain will stop falling for just a moment and then start again as heavy as ever, while the three of us gathered up our courage to go ahead and say what had to be said to Kate, do what had to be done. One of those moments in life that makes you wish you could have stayed in college forever—twenty, healthy, happy and drunk at homecoming.

Kate kept her head buried in my shoulder with her hands covering her face. She wouldn't look at us. Silent, not crying now, with every muscle in her body tightened, hard as newly set concrete, poised for the imminent arrival of ultimate horror. . . . *hurry. We'll see Father Riley tomorrow. One day more or less doesn't matter to me.* Less than an hour ago. Could that have been us?

Noah leaned forward and gently touched Kate on her shoulder. "Kate?"

"*No!*" she screamed, anger in her voice. "Go away. Get away from me. I mean it! All of you. And I mean it, too."

"Katey, Katey, my poor old Katey." Noah had tears in his eyes. But he had told her, hadn't he? In his way.

"Kate, you know me," the priest said. "It's Father Riley. Terrence Riley from Saint John's."

Silence from Kate. Absolutely no interest. He wouldn't have gotten a rise out of her at that moment if he had informed her that he was Pope Pius XII.

"I was with your mother when she died, Kate. I was holding her hand. If it's any consolation to you, she died peacefully, without pain, and in the arms of Christ. I heard her last confession and I gave her final absolution."

"Where is she?"

Father Terrence Riley looked at Noah for guidance. "They've taken her body away," Noah said. "To Hyannis. I'll take care of all that. Don't you worry about it."

"Kate, would you like for me to say a prayer with you?"

"No, thank you."

"Then I'll just say a silent prayer for her myself. Because she was a good friend and a loyal member of my parish." He placed his hand on Kate's bare head and bowed his own. Twenty seconds. "Amen. . . . She said to tell you that she loved you, Kate, that you were a good and dutiful daughter and that she knew you loved her."

"Thank you, Father," she managed to say. "And thank you for attending her." But she still wouldn't raise her head.

The priest took a small notebook and a pen from the inside pocket of his coat and wrote for a moment, tore off the page, carefully folded it and stuffed it deep inside the pocket of my parka. "I'll go now, if there's nothing more I can do. I've left my address and phone number. Please call me if I can be of any help. We . . . we need to talk about arrangements."

Father Terrence Riley got out and left us without another word and Noah took his place in the driver's seat, started the car. "I'm taking you home with me, Kate, so Dede can look after you. You'll spend the night."

Kate didn't reply. Kate was in a state of shock and Kate was still hiding out, hands covering her face, her face still buried in my shoulder. We rode in silence for a few miles. I couldn't think of anything to say and Noah couldn't either. Kate was so silent, so withdrawn that I thought perhaps she had gone to sleep. It wouldn't have surprised me. I've seen people do that when things become too much to bear, just conk out.

Finally Noah said, "Terry Riley. From Saint John's. He was on his way to give Holy Communion at a little Catholic church in West Dennis where there's no pastor. He just happened to be on the road, right there when it happened."

I reached in my parka pocket, got the note the priest had left me and read it. "Saint John's is the main Catholic church?"

"The *only* Catholic church in North Walpole. Riley's been there only a couple of years. Well liked. Comes from Boston. A Southie. Takes a real interest in the town. Without trying to run it, if you know what I mean."

I stuffed the note back in my pocket. And for some reason I can't explain, I didn't tell Noah that the priest had written something else besides his name and phone number. He had written: "Her mother also told me some other things we should talk about."

Dede Simmons, five feet two, had to hold her head back as if stargazing to look her huge husband in the eye. But there was no doubt who ran things in her house. Pretty face, cute figure, sparkling eyes, an iron-willed blue-jeans lady, The Boss, as he called her with good reason, rushed to take Kate into her arms, no argument, "Come with me right now," when we arrived at the Simmonses' home, a full, curved-roof Cape that Noah had built himself. It was like hoving into a rescue station in a storm, with Dede, of course, in full charge.

At her command, Noah called a doctor who prescribed a sedative, I don't know what, then had one of his patrolmen pick it up and deliver it from North Walpole's one and only drugstore. North Walpole had one and only one of everything.

When the officer arrived with the pills, Dede drugged Kate with authority, popped those beauties down her throat like jelly beans, take this, take this, only one more now.

It didn't take very long. Dede fluttered about like a mother bird with a new chick in the nest, explaining in detail the effect the different pills would have as she fed them to Kate, who gulped them down. Why do women love medicine so? Because they *hurt* more than men do, that's why, have more natural aches and pains. It took me a long time to figure that one out.

I sat with Kate, my arm around her, until she was yawning, her eyelids were drooping and she was slurring her words, until Dede led her away, saying, "I'll just sit with her for a while until she drops off."

"She's out and she'll be out until morning," Noah said.

"Who was in the other car? Do you know?" He had been on the phone.

"Evidently an angry young woman from the Big Apple who had words with her husband last night and was fleeing from the scene in what is now a former Porsche to her mother in Truro. Same old story. Unfamiliar with the road, driving too fast, thinking about other things. Pulled out to pass and it was all over."

I decided to leave. Kate was in good hands and there was nothing more I could do at the moment. Except go and have a talk with that priest.

Terrence Riley had been expecting me. "There you are," he said, opening his front door only seconds after I had rung the bell. "Come in out of the mist and off the moors." It was not late but already the day's light was fading. Dusk was not far away. Three-thirty on a cloudy day in winter and it's dark on the Cape.

"I read your note."

"Have you had lunch?"

"No."

"Come with me then. I was figuring on that." He had changed clothes and was dressed now in faded jeans and a gray sweatshirt which bore a Georgetown University insignia on it, dirty white sneakers. Priest at home, modern style. He led me through the rectory into the kitchen, which was a relief because the rectory looked like a cut-rate funeral home. The kitchen was much better, filled with pots and pans of all description and with lots of green plants. It was obvious he spent a lot of time there.

"Cooking's my hobby, bordering on passion," he said. "I'm like Eliot's confidential clerk. Except with me it's not pottery, it's food. How does a little gin on the rocks sound to you? In fact, you don't even have to answer the question." He made the drinks, big ones. Hit the spot, too. We both drank.

"Noah Simmons says you're doing a good job here at Saint John's."

"He does, does he?" He had a long, thick loaf of Italian bread on the kitchen counter. He cut it into thick slices and spooned some butter into a big black frying pan, and turned a flame on under it. "Not that much to it. It's like being part of a big corporation except you're a plant manager out in the boondocks."

The butter melted. He added peanut oil, mixed it in, soaked the bread slices on both sides and fried them until the bread was brown. "Don't get me wrong. It's a nice enough parish, a nice enough little town. Saint John's struggles along, trying to make ends meet. And that's not easy these days."

On a wooden board he expertly chopped capers and anchovy fillets into small bits and mixed them together. "My schools are just making it, should be better than they are. I unisexed the secondary schools five years ago. That helped some. Kate went to old Saint Ann's girls high, of course."

"Well, it's a problem all over."

He spooned more of the butter into a small saucepan, melted it, then added the capers and anchovies and cooked them, stirring occasionally. "Sometimes I think about throwing in the towel. I know I'm not destined for big things in the Church, so what difference would it make? I'm not a bad priest, mind. I don't hate the Church. I'm no rebel screaming for reform. I'm just a guy who's started thinking maybe he wound up in the wrong job, that's all."

"You're like me. You got the middle-age blahs, Father Riley."

He poured a little white wine into the saucepan, added black pepper and poured in a little chicken broth from an open can he got out of the refrigerator, then turned the flame up. "Five more minutes and we'll eat. God, I hate to hear the confessions of the dying. I've heard people confess to things they could not possibly have done. To sins which are not sins."

He placed slices of mozzarella cheese on the bread slices and slid the bread, contained on a big sheet of aluminum foil, under the broiler. "Kate's mother was in a state of shock when I reached her. But she was far from comatose."

When the cheese had melted he removed the bread from the broiler, divided the slices on two plates and poured the sauce over them. "And here we have truly adult grilled cheese." He poured white wine for us. "For your information, I am plugged in," he said. "I know all about Jane Drexel's murder. I know all about that big trust. And I know about you and Kate, Mr. McFarland."

"I don't doubt that. I'm here because of your note, that's all. It's your dime."

"I just had a funny feeling about it, a feeling that Mrs. O'Doul wasn't *confessing* anything, that she didn't believe she had *sinned*. She just wanted to tell somebody her secret before she died, to get it off her chest. If I didn't think that, I would not tell you what I'm about to."

I ate, didn't say anything. Delicious. I waited him out. He had something he wanted to say or he would not have written the note. So we ate and looked at each other, sized one another up. I decided I would have liked to have had Terry Riley the Southie on my side in any undertaking when we were both sixteen. Big and tough, there was give in him and plenty of it but you had to know where to look for it, and I didn't. Yet I knew it was there.

My play, had to. "Listen, I love Kate."

"She told me she was not Kate's natural mother."

We ate for a few moments, drank the wine, and let what had just been said sink in.

"That's what she told you?"

"As I said, not as a confession. As a statement of fact. She also told me she'd made a vow to herself to tell Kate all this after the Drexel murder was cleared up."

"What were you, holding her in your arms? You two whispering back and forth? What?"

"Elizabeth O'Doul was a dying woman. And she knew it. After all, she was an emergency operating room nurse. She told me all this in bits and pieces, as I was trying to comfort her. At times she was quite lucid. Other times, she babbled, especially toward the end. Whispered, gasping for breath, but desperate to talk. I've spent the afternoon trying to sort it out in my mind and trying to decide how much I should be telling the likes of you."

I sat there. He was going to go about it his own way.

"I know you're not Catholic. Are you a Christian?"

"I've been baptized, yes."

"Well, I guess that's something." He poured more wine for us from the jug. "I'm going to trust you, Mr. McFarland, because I have the feeling you have Kate's best interests at heart."

"I do that. I've told you I love her. I want to try to protect her."

"It's quite a story, as she told it to me. Elizabeth O'Doul, Kate's mother as we've always known her, was a young, childless widow back in 1953. A Boston native, a Navy nurse. She'd been married to a Navy fighter-pilot who was killed in the Korean War. Following his death—a carrier-deck crash—she resigned from the Navy, returned from San Diego to Boston and took a full-time job nursing and caring for Jane Drexel's old nanny, who was an invalid. Immediately after the old nanny died, Jane Drexel offered her another job, a lifetime position, that of caring for and raising a little girl, an infant described to her by Jane Drexel as an orphan. She said Jane Drexel would not say whose baby it was or where it came from. All this happened the day of the nanny's funeral, by the way. Mrs. Drexel offered her a generous salary and other benefits. Her only stipulation was that Mrs. O'Doul move here to North Walpole and raise the child here. Mrs. O'Doul knew she was barren, she was uncertain about her future, and she had always yearned for children. So she agreed. *Her* only stipulation was that the child be raised as a Catholic and that Jane Drexel play no role in bringing her up. That, essentially, is it."

"Kate thinks her father was the Navy pilot who was killed."

"And why wouldn't she? That's what Elizabeth O'Doul told her. But she told me today she never knew the identity of either the mother or the father."

"It seems obvious to me that Kate is Jane Drexel's daughter. Don't you agree? I mean, how else would the woman suddenly come up with an infant? She didn't find Kate in the bullrushes."

"No, she didn't. Which is why I decided to take you into my confidence. With this rather grand fortune at stake here, it is a delicate situation. You can see the spot it puts me in."

"Jane Drexel was a widow and really not very old. Plenty young enough to get pregnant and give normal birth. She has all the money in the world so she decides to go ahead and have the baby. She goes off somewhere under an assumed name. The child is born. Now, what's she going to do with it? And then she finds, right under her nose, a perfect substitute mother in Elizabeth O'Doul, her old nanny's nurse, a young widow, just the right age. Jane could watch the child grow up out of the corner of her eye, and still continue her elevated life-style."

"Yes, I must say it sounds pretty logical to me. What do the lawyers say? Inescapable logic."

"And I've got a pretty damned good idea who the father is, too," I said.

* * *

142

"Mac! What a nice surprise," Gerald Dickerson said when he opened his front door. "How nice of you to drop by. Come and let's go into the study. I've a fire going there."

The study was paneled with oak and there was a lovely old Bokhara rug on the floor. The fire was lively but well contained and a double window provided a good view of Wallop's Cove. A cozy room.

"How propitious," he said. He pointed at a desk which was covered with papers. "I've been working and I was just about to stop for a breather."

"You're supposed to be retired."

"It's Kate's idea. She thinks we ought to reinstitute Jane's college scholarship program. We'll choose four each year, three from North Walpole High and one from Saint John's. And with yours truly presiding once again as headmaster at an annual summer school at the cottage. I'm just going over some records provided me by both schools, weeding out the obvious."

He didn't know. I would have bet on it, hadn't been listening to the news and weather on WCIB. Somehow it would have shown on his face, in his manner. No, he didn't know about the accident, and I decided not to tell him about it until we had our talk.

I quickly inspected the study. A fussy fellow if you took a good look at it. Little things, inexpensive mementos, old souvenirs, were carefully placed. An old man's lair. He went to a sideboard and poured full portions of Kahlúa liqueur into two pony glasses.

Gerald Dickerson, I decided, had been enjoying a Sunday afternoon alone and I had disturbed his quiet nest.

"I see you got yourself some of that sweet liqueur you were craving."

"Yes, yes. Treated myself." He spread his arms. "A new cardigan. Lamb's wool. First *new* sweater I've had in twenty years." He held up his left wrist. "A digital watch, the one I told you I wanted. And I'm having the truck repaired. Just in time, I might add." Why was I calling? He never asked.

"This is a terrific house. I had the impression you were living in some cold-water, second-floor walk-up."

"The trouble is, it belongs to a wretched old woman. A widow. A miser. She's here only in July and August. The other ten months of the year it's mine."

"I don't see how you can complain about that arrangement."

"I'm house rich. That's the problem. I keep this place in perfect condition for her. She could move in any day, right now."

"It looks it."

"The gardens, the grounds. I make all the minor repairs. Maintain the place to perfection. And for that I get the use of the house. Period. I must pay the cost of the heat, electricity, all the utilities. And on my limited income the cost is staggering." He sipped his Kahlúa. I hadn't touched mine.

"I seal off most of the rooms with sheets of plastic and I turn off the individual heating units to conserve oil. This study here is my living room. I place my personal things around here when the place is mine, then pack them up and put them in a storage room and replace them with her things in late June. That's when I move into my cottage at Jane's estate. For all I do around here she *could* pay the utilities. God knows she's got the money."

"That picture?" It had caught my eye, a fading, black-and-white photograph in a frame on his desktop, a picture of four vibrant, good-looking people dressed in light summer-resort clothing. They were sitting in the cockpit of what appeared to be a huge ketch, waving at the photographer.

Gerald Dickerson picked it up, gazed at it for a moment. I had the feeling he did that often. "The summer of fifty-two. That's Chicky Koonz. My roommate at both Groton and Harvard." Mr. Koonz was a big, blustery fellow with a pleasant red face and light hair. "His wife and widow, the miser Penny." Black hair and a hard face even then. "And that's Jane, bless her." She looked enough like Kate in this picture to be her twin sister and I wondered why nobody else had noticed the obvious resemblance.

"And, believe it or not, young man, that's me." A handsome guy he had been. Dressed in white shorts, a dark polo shirt and sneakers.

"You were just a kid."

"Forty-five," he said proudly. "Fully tenured at Saint Tim's, of course. And in excellent physical condition from swimming and tennis and squash racquets during the academic year at school. Oh, yes, tip-top. Healthy as a horse."

He sat at the desk and opened a drawer. There were more pictures, contained in a small album. "Here we are. Take a look. Happy days, those."

"Chicky Koonz, your old roommate, invited you here that summer?"

"Yes. At Harvard reunion. We hadn't seen one another in years. I could tell Penny didn't exactly relish the idea of two weeks of me. But now she's getting her revenge, isn't she? No utilities! Chicky left her enough money to buy the Empire State Building."

"How did Jane come into it?"

"A friend of Penny's, classmates at Wellesley. And they both had summered here for years, of course. Jane's husband had died the winter before and she was all alone."

"She was what then? Forty-two, forty-three? And truly a beautiful woman, judging from this picture."

"Yes. Yes, she was."

"And lonely. A young widow. No children. And with all that money."

"The four of us had such a lovely two weeks together. Sailing. Swimming in Clam Pond off Jane's dock. The summer theater. Long lunches. Just such a gay time we had." He was gazing at the picture.

"So how long did it take before you and Jane were sleeping together?" He looked at me as if I'd told him his fly was open. "Come on," I said. "It shows in the pictures."

"Does it? Yes, I suppose it does."

"Don't get me wrong. I don't blame you. That was one hell of a good-looking woman."

He got up and poured himself another Kahlúa. "Yes, we were lovers that summer."

"And not just that summer. It went on for years, didn't it?"

"Yes. But we were very discreet. I truly don't think anybody in town ever suspected anything."

"Why didn't you get married? Nothing to stop you."

"I proposed. She would not accept. Perhaps she liked the intrigue. Perhaps because she basically was a loner who wanted to have me around at her own convenience."

"She must have given some reason. She never broke off your relationship."

"Oh, she'd say, 'I like it just the way it is, Gerald. It's best for both of us.' Or she would have travel plans she simply could not change. You see, Jane suffered from wanderlust. She loved to travel and did, every spring and fall, all over the world."

"You never went along?"

"Never. I was teaching, after all. And she had her set of traveling pals, a group that did not include me."

"Did she write often?"

"Never, not so much as a postcard. I never saw Jane or

146

heard from her from the end of one summer until the beginning of the next. Not a word."

"Could there have been other men? Somebody like you in Palm Beach, for example?"

"There could have been. But I don't think so."

"Why didn't you put your foot down?" I was thinking of Jane as Kate, so closely did the handsome woman in the photograph resemble the handsome woman who had me strung out like a high-tension power line. Did Kate have it in her ever to treat me with such disdain? And did I love her so much that I would take it?

The old man smiled sadly. "Because I am a pip-squeak, that's why. What would today's young people call me? A nerd?"

"You don't look like a nerd in that picture. You look like a stud."

"Looks can deceive. I spent all my productive, younger years as a teacher of boys. Does that fact suggest anything to you?"

"Are you queer? Is that what you're saying? Because if it is, I don't believe you."

"No, no. Very few private-school teachers are, despite the myth. The schools can't allow that. Most of us are people who love teaching but who are totally without ambition or drive. That's why good headmasters are so hard to find. We like the boarding school life-style, low-rent faculty housing, the quiet life, the slower pace."

There really was no polite way to pose the question. "Then what are you, exactly?"

"The bottom line? Isn't that the popular phrase? Sexually neuter. Like so many of my colleagues. Placid geldings in tweed jackets, cheering on the crew, giving advice on the production of the drama club's spring play. Sipping sherry, cheap sherry, and living on just enough money to get by. That's us, Mac."

"Are you telling me that Jane Drexel seduced you?"

"Exactly. I was handy, easy, and as you can see from the photo, strong and fit in those days. Also, dear Mac, I was a virgin, one who was teased, I might add, for my lack of experience and expertise."

"On your ass from the beginning."

He got up, walked around the room, looked out the window, then fell back into his chair. "Yes. Especially as we grew older and sex became less frequent. Her affection for me came and went. And between moments of affection there was indifference and contempt. Jane could be a shrew, believe me."

"I believe you. But you are not telling me the entire truth, are you?"

"I don't quite follow you, Mac."

"I think you do. You were quietly blackmailing Jane Drexel. For years. All that money she gave you, I don't know how much. Not presents, as you describe it. Payoffs."

He seemed to grow smaller inside the confines of the wing chair in which he sat. "I simply do not know what you are talking about."

"I'm talking about that languid summer of fifty-two when through your inexperience you managed to knock Jane up, is what I'm talking about."

He frowned in what appeared to be genuine confusion. "Knocked Jane up?"

"You got her pregnant."

He got up. "I think I'll just have a little more Kahlúa."

"She didn't travel that following fall and winter, did she? Or if she did, she didn't go very far. She went someplace nice, hid out, and had your child. And somehow you found out about it."

148

"This is absurd. Me? A father? Mac, Jane would have killed me if I'd gotten her pregnant. How did you get this farfetched notion in your head?"

"Mr. Dickerson, it's true. And you know it."

"Don't you understand, I was always terrified of the woman. She had me under her thumb and we both knew it."

"I think you're lying."

"Don't you understand, Jane never wanted a child. She was her own child, in a manner of speaking, catering to herself, pampering herself, constantly seeking new ways to please herself. She had no room in either her mind or her soul for *another* child."

"Maybe you did it and never knew about it. Did you never suspect there might have been a child?"

"No. Despite all, I loved Jane, Mac. She was the love of my life, the only person I ever had sex with. Can you appreciate that? I doubt it, the way things are today. For better or worse we were a couple. I would have known."

I gave up. And I really didn't know whether to believe him or not. "Mr. Dickerson, I have come with some terrible news, I'm afraid. Kate's mother was killed this afternoon in an auto accident on Route Six."

A look of complete dismay came over his face and the color drained from it. "Mrs. O'Doul? My lord. My poor little Katey. Is there anything I can do for her?"

"Nothing at the moment. Noah and Dede are taking care of her."

He stalked about the room, wringing his hands. I'd read about people wringing their hands in dismay, in frustration. He was actually doing it. "My poor little girl. She is so like a daughter to me in so many ways. Poor Kate. First Jane and now her mother. Are you sure there's nothing I can do?"

"I'll be in touch with you." I stood up and glanced once more at the photograph on the desk. Kate, the spitting image of her. Exactly why do you ask about a child? Do you know anything that might indicate Jane had a child? Even, where do you get off? He had not really pushed me on any of those questions. I wondered why.

There had been a child.

"I'll just walk you to the door, then," he said.

Kate's mother had told the priest that during the last moments of her life.

"I shall be in touch with Kate tomorrow," the old man said.

Maybe he *was* telling the truth, as he knew it. Maybe he had never known. "Good evening." The last words uttered by this tough, experienced investigative reporter. Hard-nosed, possessed of bulldog tenacity, famed for his probing, incisive questions. Nobody to fool around with.

I got in my rented, dented Hertz Buick and drove away.

Okay, not my best performance. But there had been a child, a baby girl born somewhere in the early spring of 1953, and handed over by Jane Drexel to Elizabeth O'Doul, who had taken her on condition, named her Katherine Mary, and raised her as her own. And a beautiful baby she would have been, too, because look at her now.

I could not, for the life of me, get a fix on Mr. Gerald Dickerson. I found it hard to believe he was the wimp he made himself out to be, who took such intolerable abuse from Jane Drexel for so many years without once striking back in anger. Was their relationship such that she could have become pregnant and given birth without the least bit of suspicion on his part? That relationship had spanned more than three decades. How could the subject of the child, *his* child in all probability, not have come up, not once, in all that time?

But neither could I believe the old man was an oppor-
tunistic scoundrel masquerading as a Caspar Milquetoast,
a greedy old bastard who had no feeling for Kate and who
had been blackmailing Jane Drexel all those years.

None of it made sense. Or, as the saying goes, did the
truth lie somewhere in between? But that didn't make any
sense either.

ELEVEN

I DIDN'T TELL KATE ABOUT IT.
Maybe later, I decided, maybe never, we'd see. Certainly it was too much to ask her to deal with at the moment.

Her mother's funeral at Saint John's was another standing-room-only affair. Kate's fame contributed to it, of course, but Elizabeth O'Doul had been a popular and highly respected emergency room nurse at Cape Cod Hospital, so the church was filled with doctors, nurses, medical technicians and secretaries, even, I was told, a few former patients.

Father Terry Riley allowed television camera crews to occupy one corner of the balcony during the funeral mass. He gave Elizabeth O'Doul her money's worth, described her as a dedicated angel of mercy, a modern Florence Nightingale.

Dede drugged Kate yet again and we carried her through the whole thing, with me holding her up on one side and Noah on the other, and with little Dede in the van. What a team. Kate sort of floated through the service. When the priest compared her mother to Florence Nightingale, she turned to me and said, clearly and placidly, "Believe you me, Mac, Jane Drexel was no Florence Nightingale." Blessed confusion.

Bascombe, Gerald Dickerson and John Norton, the other

members of that special summer club, all were there, of course, in closed ranks around Kate, standing guard. Together we carried her through it as best we could, got her through the graveside service and back to Noah's, where Dede popped more pills into her and herded her once again to bed. And again, nothing more I could do for her at the moment. So I went home.

When I got there I found a big package of mail propped against my front door, forwarded, as I had requested in a note, by a friend at my old paper in Chicago, a copy editor, a guy who wrote headlines and who tried valiantly to correct as much of the bad grammar as he could. Many of the younger reporters wrote with their fists, not their fingers. "I clean up as much of it as I can. A matter of pride," he once told me. "I couldn't possibly catch it all."

There wasn't much in the package, but what there was I savored, drawing it out piece by piece. After all, I had spent a quarter of a century in that big windy city and I won't deny that at times that winter I was more than a little homesick. I hadn't been so hungry for mail from home since I froze my ass off as a teenage Marine in Korea more than thirty years before.

There were lots of spring clothing catalogs. A few invitations to big institutional cocktail parties I never would have attended and a few invitations to events I was sorry to have missed. A letter from a young journalism graduate student at the state university who wanted to interview me for his master's thesis. A short note from the copy editor. "Here's your mail, such as it is. Don't worry. Nobody else will know your forwarding address. Where the hell is North Walpole, Ma.? Wherever, stay there because you ain't missing nothing here, pal. The barbarians are through the gates and are pillaging at will."

And a letter from Earline.

Bloodred envelope, white ink, and coyly addressed to Mr. Horace (J. J.) McFarland, who I might as well admit is the real me.

Horace. I was named after my mother's older brother, whom she had adored and I had never known. I have hated the name all my life. My newspaper byline always had been "by J. J. McFarland," my own idea and one that had seemed terrific at the young age I made it up. My friends have always called me Mac because that's how I've always introduced myself, even though in my mind to this day I can still hear my mother calling me from the back porch, "Horace! You Horace. Supper's ready!" Earline always liked to kid me about the name because she knew how much I hated it.

Here is what she wrote:

> Dear Mack, How are you these days? I am fine but I am also very sad because I am writing to inform you that our precious MouMou has passed on. I was forced to have to have her put to sleep because of pane.
>
> Well, Mack, my little fling which I am sincerely sorry for with my former employer is over, which I never felt anything for that lying twofaced Jew as I felt for you. I have changed jobs and felt more cleansed as a result.
>
> What I could really go for is a BIG MACK ATTACK! if you know what I mean.

Old Earline. Big Mack attack. Earline was horny. Well, she still had that body. She wouldn't have any trouble. I smiled at the letter, read it again. The woman didn't even know how to spell my name.

Kate hung tough, as best she could. The day after the funeral she called to say she was awake, up and about and feeling okay, all things considered. She said she was going to spend the day and night at her mother's house because there were some things she had to work out by herself. I didn't ask what things and I didn't attempt to talk her out of it.

Mothers and daughters. My son's my son 'til he finds him a wife, but my daughter's my daughter all the days of her life. And yet, Kate's relationship with her mother had not struck me as being very intense. To the contrary, my impression was that they led separate lives, working different hours in different towns, sharing only the house where they seldom saw each other. I had never met her.

I wondered why that intense love-hate relationship most mothers and daughters have did not exist. Could it have been because Jane Drexel moved in to reclaim her own after Kate's high school graduation, leaving Elizabeth O'Doul a sad and perhaps an embittered surrogate mother going her own way? People are funny.

I didn't expect her but at ten that night Kate was pounding on my door, seeking refuge. She looked like hell. "I do not want to talk," she told me as she marched in. "I just want to sleep. I can't sleep in that house for some reason."

She slept in my arms, really slept, not snoring but growling softly, the way I imagine a small, vulnerable animal sleeping in the woods would sound. I held her and thought of other things. Earline's lusty letter. A quick trip home? Fly out of Boston, surprise her with a one-night Big Mack attack, and get out of town bright and early the next morning? That was my general condition that night, not good, and with Kate, the love of my life, growling softly in my arms. I wanted a woman, not just to hold her, to have her.

I tried thinking about the story, tried to figure out which direction I should take the next day. I decided to do a little independent investigating and stop depending on Noah Simmons for information. I was as determined as ever to use the story of Jane Drexel, her murder and her wild will, to get my career back on track. So obsessed was I that I had come to think of the whole thing, the town, the victim, all the people involved, as my personal property.

I had stumbled onto it, hadn't I? The way the grizzled old prospector with the little jackass he talks to finds gold in an unlikely mountain stream. It was my discovery, my story, mine alone.

I really didn't know the territory that well, but that had never stopped me before. My motto always had been "hit the ground running" on any out-of-town assignment. You might not know the name of the street you're on but it's bound to lead somewhere and you're bound to end up knowing more than you knew when you started, nothing, if you keep asking for advice and direction along the way.

Tomorrow, I decided, I would start asking a few questions on my own. Start asking a few questions and see where they lead. Nothing wrong with that. Hell, that's what cops do. Trial and error.

I kept thinking, Where to begin? I didn't want to make a fool of myself, didn't want to lose Noah's confidence. But the time had come, and I knew it, time to push a little, time to be a little mean and insistent, time to be all the things most people don't like about news reporters. I kept thinking about that while Kate kept growling softly in her sleep like an animal in the woods.

A knock on my front door awakened me the next morning. No Kate. She had slipped out of bed without disturbing me, not the first time she had done it. She was good at it. She had left a note pinned to her pillow, "Bank business with Johnny. I'll call or you do. I left coffee." Did I fail to report that Kate, in her comings and goings, had brought over an old Toastmaster electric coffeepot which still made it and kept it hot? A good sturdy pot. I like old things that continue to work, like me.

Whoever was out there knocked again. I went to the front door to find waiting there a young man who looked like a hunter, dressed as he was in flannel-lined canvas camouflage jacket, trousers and cap.

"Morning, sir."

"No geese here. They've all flown south. They got better sense than we do."

He smiled. "My name's Pete Means. I'm a builder here on the Cape. Can I disturb you for a second?"

"Come on in. There's coffee out in the kitchen. Help yourself while I get dressed."

I like sturdy old things that keep on going, old people, old animals, draft horses or those old horses which pull carriages in the parks, old machines, old things that are stubborn, a little dirty and a little slow to get started but which go right on once they are warmed up and pointed in the right direction.

I'm also a sucker for young people who are out there busting their asses trying to make it on their own, who operate their small marginal companies and do most of the complicated work themselves at all times of day and night, especially young people who know what they're doing and take the time to do it right, who by God want that job. A vanishing breed and just the way they look makes me always give them the benefit of the doubt.

"I own a little construction business here on the Cape," Pete Means told me when I joined him in the kitchen. I liked his looks, had the minute I opened the front door to him.

I poured coffee for myself. "What can I do for you, Pete?"

"I guess I'm really not supposed to be here, not yet, but

I'd like to walk down and take a look at the property's frontage on Clam Pond."

"Sure. But why?"

"I'm going to be putting in a bid to build a dock there."

Build a dock. "Okay, why not? I'll go with you."

We walked down to the pond together. The lawn was still covered with snow but there had been a thaw and the snow had turned to mush. We sank in it as we walked and it sucked at our boots. The sun was shining. "Nice day," I said.

"Don't let it fool you. We still got a lot of winter left."

"So you're a dock specialist."

"Mister, I build anything, including docks."

"I'm new to the Cape. Still learning."

"Believe me, you're not the only new one here. Everybody in the country seems to have discovered this place in the past ten years."

"That can't be hurting your business any."

We walked to the edge of the pond. There was still a skim of ice on the surface but it was easy for the commercial clammers to break through with their long bullrakes. Three of them were out there, standing in their boats, pulling away on their rakes, trying to make a day's pay.

At low tide there was a drop of eight or nine feet from the end of the lawn down to the water's edge. "That's where the old dock went out," Pete Means said, pointing to a row of rotting wooden steps I hadn't noticed before. "Nothing left. We'd have to tear these out, rebuild from scratch."

"What would it cost in round figures to put a new dock in here?"

"You're just talking small boats. Nothing very big can get in here. Too shallow, even at high tide. Five thousand dollars maybe. But that's just the beginning of the expense. You also have to have somebody to pull the dock out of the water in the fall and put it back at the beginning of summer. Like having a gardener. Except you don't have to have a permit to grow a lawn the way you do to build a dock."

Clam Pond's ragged shore was rimmed with frozen marsh grass and lined with low-lying, gray-shingled houses, most of them summer residences which were closed and boarded up for winter, but a few of which were lived in year-round; smoke trailed up from their chimneys and drifted lazily in the air. The only sound on the pond was the rattle of clams falling into the bottom of the boats from the open iron jaws of the clam bullrakes. "A pretty place," I said.

"Everybody who comes here and buys property wants to get out on the water with a boat as soon as possible. So, if you don't exercise some control, pretty soon little saltwater inlets like this will be covered with docks."

"So getting a permit to build isn't easy."

"Try it and you'll find out."

"Take a special act of Congress?"

"Just about, if you want to build a new dock. It's a lot easier if you've got the records to prove you're only re-placing an old dock that was already there."

"Even if the dock was gone for years, the way this one has been?"

"That's right."

"Well, listen, make yourself at home. Hang around here as much as you like. I've got to get to work myself."

"Sweetie, why don't we both save ourselves a lot of time and trouble?" Betty O'Donnell suggested with a bright smile. "I know who you are and what you are. What I don't know is what you want. Make it easier on both of us."

Betty O'Donnell looked like the sort of woman who would call a perfect stranger sweetie. She smoked nonfiltered cigarettes, lighting one from another. She looked the way Earline was going to look in another fifteen years or so, and I won't add anything more to that description. Betty O'Donnell owned and operated a little real estate company out of her home, a half Cape located on the edge of town, which meant she had little or nothing to occupy her time until spring arrived.

"I need a little confidential advice, Mrs. O'Donnell."

"Ask the merchant marine where he is, the son of a bitch. Because I haven't seen him in twenty years. So I'm *not* Mrs. O'Donnell. It's Betty. So try me."

"You see, I'm really an author, a novelist, Betty. I've been working on a long novel for several years now. It took far longer to complete than I thought it would and I've used up all the advance the publisher gave me. So I've been on pretty hard times."

"What's it about?"

"Well, it's historical, based on my grandmother's diaries."

"Got any sex in it? You got to have sex, you know. I've thought about writing a novel myself, the stories I got."

"It's got enough sex, Betty, believe me. She was a pretty wild old gal." Grandma, forgive me. "Anyhow, the book is all finished now and according to my publisher I may end up with a hit on my hands, if you can believe that."

"And you may be suddenly rolling in dough?"

"Well, not rolling, Betty. The thing is, I really like it here and I'm just wondering about summer prices, is why I'm here."

"So why come to me? Why not go see Matt O'Neil? He's your buddy, isn't he? Didn't he put you in the Hollings place as a sitter? That's the way I heard it."

"Yes, but Matt's only an acquaintance. I'm thinking about staying on there next summer if my ship comes in and I need some outside, expert opinion on the rent."

"Outside, expert opinion? That's called being a consultant. Consultants don't come free."

I had been waiting for that. I gave her twenty dollars. She looked at the two tens, put them in the drawer of her desk, very businesslike, matter of fact, even though I would have bet that would be her only income for the day and maybe the week.

"You're living in a dump," she said. "An absolute dump which is going to be condemned one of these days pretty soon unless some major repair work is done, and in a hurry, which I am sure I don't have to tell you that."

"You certainly don't, Betty."

"It gets a little nicer there when the grass and the trees come in. But not much. Still, it's on the water and that counts. Tell the truth, every real estate agent in town has been eyeing that place for years, wondering what is going to happen to it. It can't just keep sitting there, not a property like that."

"What would be a fair summer-rental price?"

"It'll bring three thousand a month July and August, always has. Maybe throw in another thousand for June. For seven it's yours. Hell, offer sixty-five if you got cash. You never know."

"What if the owners decide to improve it between now and then?"

"To improve it you're talking big money. Oh, they could spend eight or nine on cosmetic improvements and hike the rental to maybe thirty-five hundred a month July and August. Maybe they'd get it, maybe not. But to really bring that old place back? It would cost a fortune and probably it'd be better just to tear it down and put in new construction. You're talking about a real relic there, my friend."

"Say they just decide to put in a new dock, for example?"

"A dock?" She laughed. "That really would be cosmetic,

like giving a rag lady a facial. Besides, the shape the place is in, I don't think they'd ever get approval."

"Thanks for the advice, Betty. Buy you a drink sometime."

"No you won't. There was a day you would have. But that was a few years back." She was right.

Matt O'Neil threw his arms up in exasperation. "How the hell would *I* know? You got to bear in mind that I am dealing with a fucking eccentric here. Sort of a Howard Hughes type. And dealing with him long distance, remember."

"I can see how that would be a problem."

"I mean we are talking about somebody who would be in the same league as Daffy Duck and Woody Woodpecker." Matt imitated Woody Woodpecker. "Know what I mean?"

"I was just curious and I happened to be in your part of town. Like I said, this young builder came by, showed up at the front door."

"Which he never should have, this still being in the diplomatic stage of negotiation, the asshole. Do me a personal favor and pay me back for giving you shelter. Keep this under your hat, will you?"

"Don't worry about that."

"Or else I'll have every old biddy in town down on me. Know what I mean?"

"I know what you mean."

"You been living there, you know what a dump the place is. While I been begging for years to spend some money on maintenance and repair. What can I do? Then a month ago or so I get this letter from out of the blue. Look into the possibility of building a new dock. The fuck?" he asked in jarhead dialect. "I just work here, know what I mean?"

"Any idea why?"

"Your guess is as good as mine."

"But I'm still okay there for the time being? No danger of getting booted out? That's what I really dropped by to ask you about."

"Enjoy. You're good until June, so long as you keep paying the utilities. The fuck, be my guest." He opened the lower drawer of his desk and pulled out a quart of Jim Beam. "Get us a couple of those paper cups over there by the coffee machine. Let's you and me have us a pop. Like they say, it must be five o'clock somewhere in the world."

Once a Marine always a Marine, so they say, and that certainly applied to Matt O'Neil. He was a big, beefy guy about my age and he had Marine Corps memorabilia on exhibit everywhere in his small office. His Purple Heart, his Bronze Star had been set in plastic and were used as paperweights. On one wall was a framed photograph of a young Matt O'Neil, lean and mean, dressed in dirty combat gear with lance corporal's stripes. At the bottom of the picture he had written, "Charlie Company 2nd Battalion First Marine Division Hill 805 June 1951." So he was the real thing, a combat veteran. I knew because I had gone up the same hill with Dog Company. It was a bitch.

He poured the whiskey and raised his cup. "Here's to our buddies who never came back," he said. Honest to God. But then he still had a crew cut. Matt was serious. We raised our cups.

"You ever think about those days?" he asked.

"As little as possible."

"I used to dream about it all the time. Still do now and then. Frozen Chosen. We deserve a goddamn memorial in Washington, Mac. Just like the Vietnam memorial, not that I begrudge them because I don't. But we should have one, too."

"Maybe one day." I drank his Jim Beam. I didn't want it but I drank it. People like Matt take offense. "You a native, Matt?"

"Naw. Wife is. I come from Pawtucket. We moved here after we were married and I was discharged, which I would have stayed in for thirty except I went out on a medical. Fifty percent disability. I tell you that?"

Yes, he had, the first night we met at the Binnacle. "Well, you look fine to me. And you obviously have a successful business."

"Cape's okay except the place closes down for the winter. To make it here you got to put lots of little things together and make hay while the sun shines in the summer and people are here with money in their pockets. In other words, you got to be a sort of entrepreneur and always keep your eye out for a new opportunity. Know what I mean?"

"Surely there's money to be made here in real estate these days."

"This? Just the tip of the iceberg, my friend. I own the Pilgrim Motel. That sandal shop on Main. Also Antiques 'n' Things, you've seen the sign. I got a summer sub shop and I run a summer lawn service, using high school kids. I'm into real estate development, getting into it. You got to put things together like that, know what I mean? And using OPM, other people's money, whenever you can, know what I mean?"

I got up and threw him a salute. "Got to go. And don't worry, my lips are sealed." I wanted out of there.

"Hey, wait a minute. Looky here." He opened the top drawer of his desk. "How long since you laid eyes on one of these?" He pulled out a Colt .45 service automatic.

"Is it for real?"

"Hell yes it's for real."

"I mean is it loaded?"

He ejected the clip. "The hell would be the reason for having a gun that wasn't loaded?" He laughed. "Some kind of fucked-up Marine you must have been, McFarland."

I laughed. He put the gun away. We shook hands and I turned to leave. On the wall, beside the door, was a framed quotation. I paused to read it.

Under fear are arranged the following emotions: terror, nervous shrinking, shame, consternation, panic, mental agony. Terror is fear which produces fright; shame is fear of disgrace; nervous shrinking is a fear that one will have to act; consternation is fear due to a presentation of some unusual occurrence; panic is fear with pressure exercised by sound; mental agony is fear felt when some issue is still in suspense.

ZENO.

"The fuck?" I asked.

"This kid in my squad, company egghead, scared shitless like the rest of us, know what I mean? He used to say that so much I made him write it down for me and got a gook to print it for me on rice paper."

"Nice."

"Who is Zeno?"

"Some Greek."

"See, this is what I think, too," Matt O'Neil said.

TWELVE

Bascombe Midgeley waved me into his office even though he was engaged in a spirited conversation with a client on the phone. His secretary was not at her desk.

"My dear," Bascombe was saying as he paced back and forth. "Stand your ground. Tell him your terms are not subject to negotiation. And stop screwing him when he comes calling without notice at midnight. Tell him, apple blossom, I keep telling you this, tell him to communicate to you through your lawyer who will talk to his lawyer. Good-bye and be good, and I mean it."

He put the phone down and sighed. "Hopeless. She's been banging everybody from Falmouth to Orleans. All you have to do is be in the immediate vicinity. And her husband has proof. But we do have to play the game, don't we? Port? That's your drink, isn't it? I think I will just have a little gin myself," he said, moving relentlessly toward his bar.

This was a Bascombe Midgeley I had never seen before, Bascombe the English country squire or Bascombe the Irish lyric poet, take your pick. Baggy tweed suit, black and blue tattersall shirt and a plaid tie. I accepted a glass of Hunting Port. He plopped two ice cubes into his glass of gin.

"I have come to pick your mighty brain," I told him.

"Snooping again, are we?"

"Talk to me about Matt O'Neil."

"What do you want to know?"

"Your impression. A profile, if you will."

"Easy. O'Neil is an ass."

"Could you expand on that a little?"

"Do you know something I don't?"

"I honestly don't know yet. Just tell me about him."

"A former Marine and wishes he were one still. I think he wants to be John Wayne. A kid from Pawtucket. He married Beverley Gochis, a Greek girl and how they met I don't know. Her parents owned and ran the Pilgrim Motel, a mom-and-pop operation. Rinky-dink but it did all right years ago when there wasn't much out here. She got it when they died."

"I don't know the place."

"You wouldn't. It's on Twenty-eight, around West Yarmouth. Seasonal. Concrete block. Postage-stamp-size swimming pool right on the highway. The Boston Irish come for a week's vacation in the summer, white as a full moon, and lie around the pool in their undershirts drinking blended whiskey from pint bottles' and chasing it with beer."

"Classy place."

"Not as classy as it once was. O'Neil's let it run down. If you can believe that."

"I gather you're not a fan of his exactly."

"He's all smoke and mirrors, old cock. A con artist. His motel's a dump. He sells third-rate merchandise in his leather shop. The antique shop is filled with junk. The kids he hires to mow lawns have a hard time collecting their last two weeks' pay. He's a drunk. He's laying some woman in New Bedford, an old girlfriend from Pawtucket. He brags about it all the time at the Binnacle bar, I hear. As for the real estate company, I wouldn't trust him to sell a chicken coop for me."

"Well, don't hold back. Tell me what you really think of the guy."

"Oh, Matt's just full of it, that's all. Talks a big deal all the time. Rides around in a Cadillac with a mobile phone. An ass."

"I think he's also a liar."

"That goes without saying." He helped himself to a tad more gin, no ice.

"Bascombe, how do you find out who owns a piece of property on the Cape?"

"It's simple. One inquires at the registry of deeds in Barnstable. The county seat. Barnstable County includes all of Cape Cod. You do know that?"

"I do now. I want to find out who owns the Hollings place."

"I can tell you that. The Hollings family."

"I'm not so sure. Make a call, will you? You must know people there."

He did, told somebody named Alicia what he wanted to know, sipped on his gin while he waited for her to look it up, made notes on a yellow legal pad, asked "When?" and "How much?" and effusively thanked this Alicia. "Well, well, *well*," he said to me.

"Well, well what?"

"How did you get onto it, may I ask? I underestimated you, McFarland. And I really must stop doing that."

"A young construction guy came to the house early this morning. Said he was going to build a new dock there. O'Neil tells me the owner, whoever that may be, wants a new dock. Betty O'Donnell, you know her, tells me building a dock there just doesn't make sense, the shape the place is in."

"It's been sold all right."

"I just had a hunch."

Bascombe glanced at his notes. "Sold about a month ago by someone named Doris Hollings Jamerson who lives in a town named Hanalei on the island of Kauai, wherever that is, in Hawaii."

"It's called the Garden Island. Hanalei is where the Bali scenes for *South Pacific* were filmed. Hell, I've been there."

He peered at me over his half-rimmed glasses. "In any event, the property was sold to a company called Clam Pond, Incorporated."

"You asked how much. I heard you."

"Yes. It's state law here that the price of a real estate sale is made public. And in my opinion Mrs. Jamerson, whoever she is, got herself a fair deal. The property sold for one million dollars. How much land are we talking about? A little more than six acres? That's about right, I would say."

"Can we find out who owns Clam Pond, Incorporated?"

"That, old cock, would be a problem. It has all the marks of a development scheme and one most probably financed by secret backers. Not uncommon around here these days."

"I have a hunch it's strictly a local deal. I have in mind an ass who talks a big deal all the time."

"Matt O'Neil doesn't have that kind of money, nothing like it."

"Maybe he borrowed it. And maybe Jane Drexel found out about it somehow and threatened to blow the whole deal. It's her bank."

He thought about it. "No. John never would have made the loan."

"And maybe O'Neil decided she had to be stopped."

"No. In the first place, John would be very close to breaking the law. He can't loan more than ten percent of his total assets on any single loan."

"At John's house, after Jane Drexel's funeral, John tried to discourage Kate when she said she wanted the trust to buy the Hollings place. Which would make sense if he knew the place already had been sold."

"Exactly what is it you're trying to get at?"

"I can't lay it out for you, Bascombe. I just have a notion that somehow, maybe indirectly, maybe not, the sale of that property is connected with Jane Drexel's murder."

"And you think Matt O'Neil did it to protect his investment."

"I think O'Neil's a wild man. And Pilgrim Bank and Trust really was Jane's bank, wasn't it?"

"Yes, I suppose it's correct to say that. We had no local bank here in North Walpole, just branch offices. Which had served us perfectly well, in my opinion. But John convinced Jane the town needed its own bank, locally owned and controlled, to serve the needs of the local people."

"So she provided the nut and had controlling interest."

"A three-million-dollar initial deposit. Three million in stock. The federal charter application breezed through. Truly a piece of cake."

"In effect, Jane established a bank for John Norton."

"No, she established a bank for herself and hired John to run it for her. After Yale Johnny went to Wharton. He was working as the assistant manager at the First Boston branch here when Jane decided to launch Pilgrim. He did all the groundwork. I made the application for the charter."

"But you said the bank was John's idea."

"Yes. You've got to understand, Johnny grew up around banking. His mother was chief teller for years at Cape Cod Five. A widow. When he was a kid he worked after school there as a janitor and as a messenger, a handyman. Destined to be a banker from birth."

"Mr. Arithmetic."

"You see, it's John's belief that a little town here on the Cape has got to have its own bank, locally owned and supported, if the town is to ever have its own, complete identity. He convinced Jane that North Walpole would remain a village, not a true town, without its own bank. So now we have ourselves one. Pilgrim is his entire life, of course. He's there day and night, often until past midnight."

"Dedication and attention to detail. All the how-to books say that's the real secret to success."

"Hard work," Bascombe agreed. "Johnny's a hard worker."

"Don't get me wrong, Bascombe. I like him, too. A lot."

"He and I grew up here together. He was the widow's boy and I was the son of the minister who had to clerk in the hardware store to make ends meet. We played together as kids, went to school together, church."

"You two were more than members of a group. You were best friends."

"We have been, all our lives. Even though he was always special and I was ordinary, the kind of kid who comes in second, or third, never first but never quite last either."

"Oh, come off it, Bascombe."

"At the living Christmas pageant in the park, who was Joseph? John was, of course. And who was a lowly shepherd? Yours truly. On the high school baseball team? John pitched. I was the catcher. On the football team? John was the kid who stood there tall and cool at quarterback, scouting up and down the line while he barked the count. With his hands jammed up my crotch. I played center. He was senior class president, of course. I was secretary."

"And on top of everything else, he's a good-looking guy."

"Listen, when we were in grade school the teachers used to pet him. They couldn't help themselves, couldn't keep their hands off him. In high school every good-looking girl in our class used to sob herself to sleep, clutching old stuffed animals, when Johnny asked somebody else to go to the movies. Me, I got my hand on one tit, and I had to go steady with her for two years to manage that, old cock."

Bascombe walked over and helped himself to a little more gin. I waved no when he lifted the bottle of port.

"I'm a bit overweight now," he said. "Drink too much. But as a youth I was not physically repulsive, not by any means. No bad teeth, or an unfortunate nose, or a chin that disappeared into my shirt collar. I was not a fatso, not in those days. Sturdy, and ordinary looking. I didn't put the girls off but neither did they take one look at me and go bananas."

"But John Norton was the prince of the Cape."

"Handsome, graceful and popular. Not in any way conceited. A decent guy who never thought of himself as being anything special so we didn't either. Yet we knew he was. He was always included. Never left out of anything. Always picked first."

"Jack Armstrong, the All-American Boy."

"I know he comes close to being a pain in the ass at times, the way he plays the town booster. But it's not an act with him. He truly loves this town and the people in it. And the people here know it. And love him for it."

"I believe that."

"He sees himself as a public servant. We've had talks about it. And I must say, his brand of go-go banking seems to be successful."

"Bascombe, you paint a picture of a man without an enemy in the world."

"I really don't think he has one."

"A real workaholic, however."

"He has to be. Starting up a brand-new bank, especially in a small town and especially in these days of deregulation, it's not easy. It's like raising a child from infancy. You must feed it, make it grow to some size, and then it can do all sorts of helpful things, run and jump, fetch the paper, carry out the garbage. The difficult thing is, you've got to attract new depositors *and* new, reliable loan customers at the same time. Trying to do just that is what keeps old Johnny on the run all the time. The bank's only three years old, you know. Still just a baby."

"Is he making it?"

"It will never come close to being the dominant bank on the Cape. But, then, it's not meant to be that. It's meant to be *North Walpole's* bank. Part of the town's heart."

"Bascombe, if I can ask, what's your own personal involvement?"

"None. At least not yet. I'm not on his board and he never discusses figures with me. But he seems to be doing okay. I know Jane Drexel had no complaints. And, after all, most of it was her money."

"Which now belongs to The North Walpole Trust."

"Correct. In effect, Pilgrim now belongs to the trust, which owns about seventy percent of its stock."

"So you would expect to be named to the board."

"I will demand to be named to the board, old cock." He took a look at his watch, a gold pocket watch with a lid, of course. "Are you going to the party? Best we bundle up and be off."

"What party? I haven't been invited to any party."

Bascombe laughed. "Of course you're invited. Everybody in town is invited."

"Where? News to me."

"At the bank, where else? Two o'clock. Johnny's been calling people all morning. Spur-of-the-moment thing. Typical of him. He says it's a thank-you party."

THIRTEEN

T HE JOINT WAS JUMPING WHEN
I got there. The teller cages had been closed and no business was being conducted, but the main banking floor was
filled with people. Sure enough, Pilgrim Bank and Trust
was giving a party. The six or seven women who worked
there were dressed as if they were going to a wedding.
They greeted you at the door with big smiles of welcome,
even if they didn't know your name.

John Norton was playing host and I thought I had seen
few men who looked happier in the role. The cowboy on
horseback riding home to the cabin with the Christmas tree
in tow, the hunter with his frantic dogs just loosed in the
autumn field, the contented drunk on his regular stool at
his favorite bar. And Johnny Norton standing on the floor
of his bank welcoming his guests, his customers, the towns-
people of North Walpole.

"Mac! Welcome. So glad you could make it," he said to
me, offering his hand. White shirt, navy-blue suit, a red
carnation in his lapel, and a big smile on his face. Sign the
kid up, the Paramount casting exec would have said. With
looks like that, we'll teach him how to act. A perfect Mr.
Nice Guy.

After my talk with Bascombe I had made a phone call
to an old friend in Honolulu whose first words to me, of

course, were, "McFarland, don't you know what time it is out here?" We had covered the Tet offensive together back in '68 and now he was managing editor of the *Star Bulletin*. I told him it was urgent so he called his stringer in Hanalei, in the middle of the night, and was told that Doris Hollings Jamerson was a fading lady of a certain age with a fondness for vodka and pineapple juice who was married to a much younger man of questionable means and origin. At first, when they moved there, there had been money to burn, which they had proceeded to do. Followed by hard times, until recent weeks. Now they were sporting around in a new BMW and were on a nonstop credit card binge. And back on the vodka.

"This is not the way banks do business where I come from," I told John Norton. I took a look around. Noah, in uniform. I raised my hand in greeting. Bascombe was gulping champagne and eating a late lunch of finger sandwiches. No Matt O'Neil.

"That says to me that banks where you come from have a lot to learn about modern banking," John said. He took me by the arm. "Come on. There's somebody I want you to meet."

He led me across the room to where a big mahogany table was placed along the wall and covered with a white-linen tablecloth. At one end there were plastic cups and several open bottles of champagne, a Bollinger brut, a Moët & Chandon White Star, an Iron Horse brut, a Schramsberg blanc de noirs, as if he had called the liquor store and told them to ice up and send over every decent bottle they had in stock.

At the other end of the table a woman sat pouring tea from a big, ornate silver pot, a thin, handsome woman in her sixties with silver hair who wore a well-cut black wool dress, a pearl necklace and gold earrings. "Mother, I want you to meet a friend of mine Mr. McFarland," John said to her.

She smiled at me graciously. "I'm Helen Norton, Mr. McFarland. Will you have milk or lemon?"

"Or champagne?" her son asked.

"Lemon, please. No sugar."

"Just the way I take it." She poured.

"Mother lives in Brewster, in a new condo community there. Sarah and I don't see as much of her as we'd like."

Helen Norton looked at him as if he were a fresh cinnamon-raisin bun still warm from the oven. "Any more and I'd be making a nuisance of myself, dear."

"I understand you have a few years' experience in the banking business yourself," I said to her.

"I just took it in, counted it, and paid it out. That's about all they would allow women to do in my time."

"I guarantee you she'd be running things if she was around today," John said.

Kate and Sarah walked up. Kate brought a fresh pot of tea and John's wife carried a big platter of cucumber sandwiches. Kate was all dressed up, gray suit, white blouse, wearing her contacts. Prettiest woman in the room, no contest. She squeezed my arm. "Have I got news for you," she whispered.

John placed a hand on her shoulder. "This is the person who should be the guest of honor today. Have you told Mac, Katey?"

Kate blushed. Kate was excited. "Actually, they're naming me to the bank's board of directors."

"It's only proper, considering the trust and the new position of responsibility Kate holds," John said, giving her a hug.

A plump blonde, maybe forty, came skipping over, squealing for a hug and a kiss from John, who accommodated her. She led him away by the hand, saying he just had to meet two friends of hers from Falmouth. "Business, excuse me," John said to us with a big smile on his face.

It was a nice party, a friendly gathering. It was obvious that the people from Falmouth were just about the only people in the room John didn't know, and it was equally obvious that everybody there was as fond of him as he was of them. Even though, in such a small town, they ran into each other almost every day, the party almost was like a homecoming, a reunion of people who hadn't seen each other for years, with hugs and backslaps and shouts of recognition as John drifted away from the people from Falmouth and cruised the room, greeting and joking with them all. John seemed to bring that out in people.

"Why, Arthur, how nice to see you," Helen Norton said to a man who had come for tea.

"Afternoon, Helen." He was her age, more or less, dressed in gray flannels and a tweed jacket, a stocky man whose bearing said Town Leader. "And, young lady, it's going to be a pleasure having you join us on the board," he said to Kate, who introduced us. He was Arthur Tyleston and he owned a building-supply center out on Route 28. "The largest on the Cape," Kate said. "It says so on the sign."

"Arthur was a good customer of mine for twenty years at Cape Cod Five," Helen Norton said. "Until John took him away."

"At least I kept it in the family, didn't I? That boy of yours is really something, Helen. You have every reason to be proud of him."

"He's always been a good boy, hardworking and anxious to please. You know his father died before John was old enough to walk, so he just grew up helping out, lending a hand. He never gave me a moment's trouble or cause to worry, Arthur."

"Well, I wouldn't go quite that far myself," Sarah said. "I can't get him to slow down, much less stop for a second. It's seven days a week with John. This bank is his entire life, I swear."

"Good bankers must pay meticulous attention to detail," Helen Norton said. "John's father was a certified public accountant, you know. Worked himself to death."

"But, I mean, when we went to Maui I had to bind and gag Johnny to get him on the plane. And he was on the phone to the bank at least once a day. And this *party*. He calls me this morning from out of nowhere and informs me he's entertaining half the town in two hours' time."

Helen Norton's eyes blazed briefly. A steel mill furnace door opened for a moment, then slammed closed. She shook her head sadly. "If only the two of you could have had children of your own."

Sarah wasn't having any of it, not for a second. "Helen, it really wouldn't have made any difference. Remember, I've known him since I was eighteen myself."

Arthur Tyleston sighed. "I don't know what North Walpole would do without John, him and a few others like him. So many of our best young people grow up here and then move away. It's nice to have a few like him to stick around and run things. We old-timers aren't going to last forever."

"Boy, isn't that the truth," I said. Foolishly. I didn't mean it the way it sounded, smart-ass. When I was around Kate I tended to run off at the mouth. She put her arm around my waist, gave me a sharp pinch on the rib cage and smiled at me sweetly.

"All of you gather around me," Arthur Tyleston said. "I've got a little secret and it's time I let all of you in on it. You probably know I'm president of the chamber of commerce."

"I didn't," I said and Kate pinched me again. "I mean, I'm sort of new in town."

"Our annual banquet's next month and I know I don't have to tell you that our award of Man of the Year is our closest held secret. It's the single greatest honor the chamber can bestow."

"I have a feeling I'm going to have to go to Boston and find a new dress," Sarah said.

"Indeed you must. And you, too, Helen. John's by far the youngest man ever to win the award. A unanimous choice, too. Now I'm swearing all of you to secrecy. But I know you women need a little time in advance to get fixed up for an occasion like this."

"He will love it. He will just love it," Sarah said. "I'm going to get him a new dress shirt at Brooks in Boston. Oh, God. He is going to be so happy."

"Excuse a mother's pride, but it's not as if he doesn't deserve it," Helen said.

"Remember, not a word," Arthur Tyleston said.

"What is this, a conspiracy? What are you people cooking up here?" John had made his way back to us.

"Oh, nothing, darling," Sarah said. She was glowing, so happy was she for her Man of the Year.

I'm no psychic. I have no built-in early warning system. But I'm old enough to know trouble when I see it coming, and I saw it coming at that very moment in the form of two men who were making their way across the crowded bank floor to our group. They were a mismatched pair. One of them was tall, thin and impeccably dressed and the other was stocky and disheveled. But they had one thing clearly in common. Both had looks of anger and anxiety on their faces. They were almost but not quite shoving people out of their way to get to us.

179

"*There* you are, Whitney," John said to the taller man when they reached us. "And right on time, too."

"Johnny, what in the name of God is this?"

"No problem. Just a little customer party. My word on it. Meet Whitney Snow," he said to the rest of us. "We roomed next door to each other for four years in college. I went on to become a modest small-town banker. And Whitney here has gone on to become the new bank commissioner of the state of Massachusetts."

"John, you should not have done this." The man's face was chalk white and he spoke to John Norton as if the rest of us were not there.

"And this must be your friend from the comptroller's office."

"I'm Robert Hertgen, Mr. Norton. And I must tell you, this is highly irregular."

"Bob's just flown up from Texas," Whitney Snow said. Bob looked it. His face was gray and haggard and his suit looked as if it had been slept and worked in for several consecutive days and nights and then flown in. Bob Hertgen looked as if he were about to pass out from exhaustion. The tip ends of him were quivering, fingers, lips, eyelids, the twitch of total fatigue. A tired hit man on overtime. He coughed into a tissue.

"Johnny, what is going on here?" Sarah asked anxiously. Wives know trouble, good ones do. They can see it coming, see it out of the corner of one eye.

John gave her a quick, ressuring hug and a kiss on the cheek. "Not to worry, sweetheart. The mean old feds have dropped in to take a look at our books, that's all. Pour them some champagne. I'm going to make a little toast. Be right back."

"Johnny, come back here!" Whitney Snow shouted. Quite beside himself. Stamped one foot on the carpet in his frustration. The problem of dealing with old friends in trouble when suddenly you're the guy in charge. I felt sorry for him.

Johnny bounded across the banking floor, pushing people aside, jumped on top of a loan officer's desk and spread his arms. "Quiet, please. Could I have your attention, please?" Conversation quickly ceased and people gathered round.

"Commissioner, you got to stop this," Hertgen said and sneezed into his tissue.

"Let's give him a minute or two."

John was on stage and he looked like a million dollars, could have been hosting *The Price Is Right* or, for that matter, the Miss America contest. All smiles and waves, and nods of recognition. He might have been presenting the awards at the county fair. "I want to thank you all for coming," he said. "And I especially want to thank the team from Joe Falleta's North Walpole Liquors who did such a fine job of getting the wine on ice and delivered right on time."

There was applause.

"You cleaned us out, you son of a gun," Joe Falleta called out. "We ain't got a decent bottle left in the store. And wait till you get the bill!"

"How long has he known?" Bob Hertgen asked Whitney Snow.

"I told him at noon, the time you and I agreed on. I never thought he would pull something like this."

"I'm simply suggesting we have a potentially difficult situation here. A whole room full of customers. Anything could happen, that's all." He sneezed, sneezed again. His tissue was wadded and sodden. He tossed it into a wastebasket. Whitney Snow produced a linen handkerchief and gave it to him. Hertgen nodded in gratitude and blew his nose, a big honk. "Jesus, I'm dying. Goddamn airplane full of service kids and I had a middle seat. It's a wonder I don't have pneumonia and maybe I do."

John raised a plastic glass of champagne someone had given him. "A toast. First to my mom. The best banking brain on the entire Cape. I guarantee you that. And to my wife, Sarah. You all know Sarah. She's my partner. She made the cucumber sandwiches you all are enjoying today."

"John made straight A's in public speaking at North Walpole High," Helen Norton said to me. "He also was captain of the debating team that went to the state finals. He would have been wonderful as a television anchorman."

"I haven't been home in seven weeks," Bob Hertgen said to Whitney Snow. "I don't even know if I got a wife left. To hell with the overtime." He sneezed again into the linen handkerchief. "Look, I got no choice, commissioner. I'm going to go out now and call in my team. You've got to understand my position in this."

Whitney Snow sighed, closed his eyes for a moment, then nodded yes, reluctantly, the way a prison warden with doubts would signal *fry*. Hertgen turned and left.

"I see a lot of old friends here," John Norton said. "For example, there's Mrs. Adams, who's going into the jam and jelly business, using a loan we've arranged for her."

"Yes, after I promised to keep him supplied with my wild beach plum jelly for the rest of his life," Mrs. Adams said. She looked like Aunt Bee in Mayberry.

"And I see Father Terrence Riley over there, sampling the bubbly. I'm honored to say that Saint John's banks with us. And both Father Terry and I do love to see those bingo receipts come in, right, Father Terry?"

The priest raised his glass. "There's Irish blood there somewhere!"

"Johnny. Johnny. Why are you doing this to yourself?" Whitney Snow muttered.

"And we have a god present with us in this room today,"

182

John said. "We all watched him grow up, sensing greatness even then. Jimmy Olsen's greatest ever Little Leaguer. The Cape's greatest high school football player. Ever. Boston College's greatest offensive tackle. Ever. And last year's first-round draft choice of the New England Pats. And might I just add with no little amount of pride, a customer of this bank. Need I say the name? Buppy Santos!"

A horse with no neck, Buppy raised one arm as high as he could in salute. Muscle-bound Buppy.

The members of Hertgen's closing team had quietly entered the bank, about twenty young, sober-faced men and women, most of whom were carrying portable computers. Hertgen, the handkerchief held to his nose with his left hand, waved them into position with his right. They moved quickly, taking their places in front of all the teller cages and at every door that led to the offices in back, the doors which led to the safe and to the vaults where deeds and mortgages, trusts and loan papers and all the accounting records were kept. Young, but you could tell, tough, experienced professionals.

"I want to thank you all for coming to the party," John told the crowd. "It's our way of saying thanks for all your support. And now I bid you all good afternoon. This bank will be open for business as usual at ten o'clock Monday morning." He jumped off the table and headed for the front door to shake hands with his departing guests.

I approached Whitney Snow. "You're not going to be very happy to see this," I said and showed him my *Globe* press card.

"Good Christ, you're all we need. How'd you get onto this?"

"Entirely by accident. I haven't even phoned the paper about it yet. But it's going to be public knowledge within hours. You know that."

"You're right."

"You're closing this bank, aren't you?"

"That is correct, I'm afraid. The comptroller of the currency is declaring the bank insolvent. Bob Hertgen's the closing manager for the F.D.I.C."

"What happens now?"

"Just as soon as these people leave I'm going to get the employees together and tell them the bad news that Pilgrim Bank and Trust no longer exists. John already knows. That's why he gave the party. It was a farewell party."

"He said the bank will be open for business as usual on Monday."

"Not quite as usual. It will be open as a new branch of the First National Bank of Falmouth. They've agreed to pay half a million for the franchise and to buy six million worth of loans and other assets."

"What went wrong?"

"Too many bad loans. Johnny loaned more money than he took in. He couldn't say no. He was warned, too. The F.D.I.C. put him on their list of troubled banks a couple of months ago."

"What about the depositors?"

"All accounts of one hundred thousand or less are covered by F.D.I.C. insurance, of course. Over that, they'll have to wait until this closing team liquidates the assets Falmouth First didn't buy." He paused. "Johnny had to go to the money brokers to raise cash to pay interest on deposits. That was the final warning flag the feds just couldn't ignore."

"The stockholders?"

"They will lose it all."

"What about Johnny?"

"Do you mean, is there a chance he'll be charged with a crime? I don't know. God, I hope not. There's going to be enough trauma as it is. Don't print that, please."

"What happens now?"

"The F.D.I.C. takes over. It's their bank now. This team hid out in a Hyannis motel last night, posing as a conference of insurance salesmen. Now they'll seal everything, count the cash, conduct an audit, and try to cut the federal government's losses as much as they can by collecting on as many loans as quickly as they can. It's a federal affair. I'm really just a bystander, required to be here by law."

"They don't mess around, do they?"

"They don't exactly enjoy their work, you know. Bob Hertgen just finished closing a bank in a little oil town in west Texas and got sent here. Bone tired. They all are. They've all come from other closings."

"The news of this is going to hit this town like a bombshell."

"Don't you think I know that? I don't enjoy this part of my job. This . . . well, damn it, this is my first closing. I don't relish it."

"I wouldn't either."

"Hertgen's warned me. There's going to be a whole lot of crying and gnashing of teeth in here a few minutes from now when I tell the staff their bank's gone under."

Paws up, I thought.

John Norton was still standing at the main entrance, shaking hands, taking just a bit too long to tell everybody good-bye. "I like that guy," I said.

"He's almost like a brother to me," Whitney Snow said. "You don't know."

"I've had a couple of friends like that. They're hard to come by."

"If I regained consciousness on the streets of Calcutta, sick, and had only one dime in my pocket and there was a pay phone I could crawl to . . ."

"You would call John Norton."

"And he would come get me. I know he would. That's the point."

"How the hell could he have made such a mess of things?"

"He had too many friends on the streets of Calcutta who made that call, I suspect. We won't know until the audit's completed. You know, with a small bank such as this sometimes all it takes is a few bad big loans."

"Well, I'm worried about him. Wouldn't you say he's acting a little strange. Weird? This party. Knowing what's coming, about to happen."

"He's trying to put if off as long as possible, I suppose. The poor son of a bitch."

To hell with the story. I had to get out of there, not run but walk briskly to the nearest exit before the fire alarm went off. I didn't want Kate to witness John Norton's humiliation. It's called running away from reality and at times there's nothing wrong with that, a lot to be said for it, in fact. Get the hell out while there is still time. Sometimes that's how people live to tell the tale.

I got Kate and Sarah got her mother-in-law. Johnny, still smiling and as cheerful as ever, kissed all three of them and shook my hand.

"You all go along," he said. "The feds are going to be doing an audit here."

Sarah asked, "Johnny, is everything all right?"

He laughed. "Ask Mom to explain it to you. And don't wait supper for me because it's going to be a long night."

I thought he looked like a fit athlete about to run a race he believed he had some chance of winning, at least willing and ready to give it his best. You wanted to wish him good luck before you took your seat in the stands.

"Those federal audit teams are nitpickers, believe me. They drive you crazy. And I know from experience," Helen Norton said. She gave her son a hug and another kiss. "Johnny, you certainly had yourself quite a party."

186

FOURTEEN

A NEW COLD FRONT WAS MOV-
ing in from the west, just as the Weather Wizard on WCIB
in Falmouth had predicted, a solid, foreboding line of cloud
which looked like a long, low black wall to the west set
against the clear blue sky we had enjoyed all that day.
"Button up your overcoats, folks, and get out those snow
shovels. One more time!" That had been the Weather
Wizard's advice on drive-time radio, and right on the
money it was, too. By the time Kate and I pulled into the
driveway of the Hollings place the first few flakes were
blowing in.

I quickly threw a fire together, I had the technique down
pat by then, and poured us some cold ginger ale, which
was the best I could come up with that chilly evening.
Besides, Kate had had more than enough champagne at
the party, forget about the quart of vodka I had in the
kitchen. I also had Ritz crackers, a hunk of sharp cheddar
cheese and a jar of pimento peppers. More than enough.
We ate and drank in silence.

She sat on the couch with MouMou snuggled in her lap.
The dog's old, weak eyes were pearly gray and glazed with
age, looked like two tiny oysters set in her balding old head,
but still filled with hatred as she glared at me. We would
never get it together, this dog and I.

"Okay, class is in session," Kate decreed, wrapping her

skirt around her legs. "Something funny is going on here and I want to know what the hell it is." Full of herself, the new member of the non-bank's board of directors.

"They've closed the bank, Kate."

"What do you mean, *closed* the bank? And who are *they*? What *is* this? The feds are doing an audit, that's all. Johnny said."

"Look, I don't want to have to explain it twice. It's getting late. So just sit and listen while I dictate my story to the paper, okay?"

She did that, listened without comment and with growing consternation while I did my work. By the time I finished dictating my story she had her head in her hands.

And, while I am at it, will somebody please explain to me why it is that bad news is so much easier to report than good news. No doubt because bad news usually is so brutally simple and without complication, easy to state. President shot. Wall Street lays an egg. North Walpole bank fails.

Kate listened, stroked MouMou, while I talked with Dave Farkas, who listened to a replay of the dictated copy and then came on the line to praise my initiative and enterprise and my unique knack for being in exactly the right place at the right time. He said he would have another reporter from the business section check around and insert into my story any additional information he might come up with. Page one, of course. Above the fold.

Kate listened, stroking the old dog's back, while I kept saying "Great, great" and "Thanks a lot" and "Let me get back to you on that one tomorrow" as Farkas told me he was giving me a byline on the story and to hell with company policy, that he had checked things out with the paper's managing editor and I had a full-time job as a staff reporter waiting for me anytime I wanted to come to Boston to fill out the personnel forms.

Give me your best opinion. Do you think I hung up that phone and turned to Kate and told her the good news? Told her that I had managed finally to reclaim my professional life, put it all back together, that through honest effort I had restored my sense of self-confidence, my self-respect? I said nothing of the sort.

Kate looked at the fire as she thought about the story I had dictated. "Poor Johnny."

"My ass. Bascombe told me Jane Drexel sank around six million bucks into that bank to get it started up, money that would have belonged to the trust now. Now it's all gone. Poor Johnny blew it away, Kate. So don't 'poor Johnny' me."

"I confess, I really don't understand what's going on."

"Kate, John Norton could end up going to jail. For any number of reasons, including bank fraud. That's what's going on. God only knows what the feds will find when they do the audit. Because short of your typical banana-republic dictator and the governor of the state of Louisiana, nobody has more total authority than the president of a typical small bank. It's his money to use as he sees fit."

"You're accusing him of being a crook."

"This place here has been sold. You didn't know that, did you? Sold right under your nose for a million dollars to something called Clam Pond, Incorporated. My hunch was the new owner is Matt O'Neil. Now I think Johnny may be in on it, too. I don't know that for a fact, just a guess and I hope a bad one." I had turned on only one table lamp. The uneven light from the fire cast shadows on Kate's face. It sounded like it was sleeting outside, or something.

"Johnny was the first boy I ever had a real crush on," she said.

"Sometimes people change. Without realizing themselves that they're changing. You drift into things, settle into ways and routines. You form new habits, start taking things for granted. And when they blow the whistle on you, you say, 'Hey, wait a minute, I wasn't doing anything wrong. Just normal operating procedure.' "

"Mac, I don't want to hear any more about it."

"Because you know what I'm about to say next. Noah was at the bank this afternoon. Noah's not stupid. Noah is very, very intelligent. What do you suppose Noah's thinking right now?"

"I'm not going to sit here and listen to this."

"Noah's thinking maybe John Norton could have killed Jane Drexel. That's what."

"No! Johnny could never have done such a thing."

"Kate, I spent a quarter of a century writing about things like this. You wouldn't believe what people, ordinary people can do. And then lie about it. Cover it up. Pretend it never happened. I'm just laying out the worst possible case, that's all. We've got a guy in big trouble here."

"And you love it, don't you?"

"What's that supposed to mean?" I knew what she was getting at. I just didn't like hearing her say it.

"You should have heard yourself on the phone. Great, great. Thanks. Big story. That's all it is to you."

"That's a mean thing to say, Kate."

"But it's true. We're all just somebody to write about. But Johnny's a real person to me. I love him. I still let him kiss me," she said defiantly. "You didn't know that, did you? Sometimes. Sometimes when Sarah's not around he kisses me, Mac."

"So what? Do you think that matters to me?" I stalked out to the kitchen, found the quart of vodka and drank from it as if it were a Boy Scout canteen. I was stunned with jealousy and anger. My chest was tight and I had a dry and bitter throat.

"Mac?" she called to me from the living room.

"Do you think that matters to me, Kate? Kiss who the hell you want to kiss. Kiss my ass while you're at it."

"Mac, come out here, please."

"I ought to throw you out of here, Kate."

I marched back into the living room. Kate still sat on the couch and the fire I had built was blazing nice and high. Johnny Norton was standing there, just inside the front door. He had a big gun in his right hand.

Johnny was a mess. He still wore the dark-blue suit he had worn at the party and the red carnation was still in his lapel. He wore no topcoat, no hat, and his head and shoulders were covered with a sprinkling of sleet which melted quickly from the heat of the fire. The right side of his coat and the front of his shirt were soaked with blood. You couldn't help but notice it. Also, he held the barrel of a Colt .45 pressed firmly against his right temple. You couldn't help but notice that, either.

I think back about it and I think all three of us on that cold evening of that suddenly sullen day were surprised and shocked but, most of all, confused and *embarrassed*, deeply embarrassed, to find ourselves caught in this situation.

I said, as evenly as I could manage, "Hello, John. Nice to see you." Nice to see you? He had this fucking gun the size of a fat old whore's thigh pressed against the side of his head, all set to blow himself away. And us as well if he was of a mind to do it.

"Oh, *Johnny!* Put it *down!*" Kate wailed.

"I've got to talk to you, Kate. There're some things you must know."

"Not with that gun in your hand. Please. Mac, make him."

No sweat. "John, Kate and I are going sit here on the

couch together. Why don't you sit in that chair across from us and you can talk to Kate all you want."

I sat down beside her on the couch and put my arm around her shoulders, trying to appear nonchalant, but determined to keep her by my side and not under any circumstances allow her to run to the man with the gun. Who might decide to press it to her head. John hesitated for a moment, then sat in the chair. But he kept the gun barrel pressed to his head. He let out a deep breath. *"Boy,"* he said.

"Johnny? Honey, we can get it straightened out." She made a sudden effort to rise but I tightened my grip around her shoulders.

"The bank's gone, Kate. It doesn't exist anymore. And I guess I don't either."

"John, I want to suggest something," I said. "You're making Kate very nervous holding that gun against your head like that. Me too, frankly. Because the damn thing could go off. So why don't you lay it on the table beside you? That way we can all relax and Kate and I won't be so nervous, okay?"

"Oh. Sure. Sorry." Just like that. Jesus, what an insane afternoon this was.

"Mac thinks you and Matt O'Neil bought this place."

"Yes, we did. I won't apologize for that. Matt spent months putting this deal together. I told you, Kate, development here can't be totally stopped. Not even with all of Jane Drexel's money. My idea was six detached houses. One-acre lots. Cape style. Architect designed. Keeping all the trees so you couldn't even see the houses from the road. Barely from the pond. With one common dock strictly for small boats."

"I can see that. I don't think that's such a bad idea," Kate said.

"I only wish I had some plans to show you what I had in mind."

"I think I've got the general idea. Oh, *Johnny!*"

"The woman who owned it is a hopeless old drunk who Matt said was ready to sell to anybody who would meet her price. I didn't want outsiders getting control of it."

"One million dollars," I said.

"A fair price. You've got to understand. Matt put everything he owned up as collateral on the loan. His home, the motel, everything. He looked at this as his one big chance. I loaned him eight hundred thousand."

"So you were in for two," I said. A guess.

"With my own house as collateral. It's worth half again as much as that in today's market."

"You loaned *yourself* money, Johnny?"

"Nothing wrong with that, Kate. Bankers do it all the time. Mac will tell you."

"He's right," I said. "Usually it's best to have approval from your board of directors. And didn't the loans put you over the bank's legal lending limit, Johnny? You were cooking the books, weren't you?"

"I could have straightened it out if I'd had a little more time, three or four months, that's all. I'd extended too many loans, to guys who'd run into some bad luck. There was a sudden glut of condos on the market last summer that wouldn't move. I ran short."

"Why are your clothes so bloody, Johnny? You are covered with blood." Kate could have gone all night without saying that, but say it she did.

John looked at me. "There's been an accident. *Boy.*"

"That's Matt O'Neil's gun you've got, isn't it?"

He looked at it. "Yes." I was sure it was the same Colt .45 Matt had shown me earlier that day in his office. John rubbed his eyes with his fists. *"Boy!"* So handsome he was,

193

even then, like a matinee idol made up to appear dirty and weary from battle in a World War II movie. "Matt missed the party at the bank. There's some woman in New Bedford he sees when her husband's away. He was with her all afternoon, drinking and screwing, I guess you'd say."

"I guess you would," Kate said.

"He didn't learn about the bank's closing until he got back from New Bedford and stopped at the Binnacle. It was all over town by then, of course. He called me and asked me to meet him in his car out in the bank parking lot."

"Which obviously turned out to be a big mistake," I said.

"He was drunk, drinking whiskey straight from a quart bottle. Drunk and crazy. He wanted me to go inside and get his loan and mark it paid in full. When I told him I couldn't do that even if I wanted to, he pulled this gun. Threatened to kill me."

"You tried to take it away from him and it went off."

"Yes. Exactly."

"John, is he dead?"

"I think so. I just got out, got in my own car and drove away. Scared. I still am. I'm scared, Mac. I've got the shakes, for the first time in my life. Look at me."

I gave Kate a hard look to put her on hold. "It sure sounds like a clear case of self-defense to me."

"It was. I swear it. He would've killed me. The man was out of his mind. Drunk. He wasn't making sense. He blamed me for everything."

"I know what I'd do. Go straight to Noah. Right now. It'll look better that way."

"Look at me, Mac. I'm a mess. Blood all over me."

"Then why not call him? The phone's right there on the table."

He looked at it as if he had never seen a telephone before. But he was about to pick it up.

194

"Johnny, there's something I've got to ask you," Kate said.

"No she doesn't. You don't have to ask John anything, Kate."

"Yes I do."

"Let John make the call to Noah first, then ask him."

"Mac thinks you killed Jane. Did you?" Just like that.

John Norton looked at me for a long time. "No, I didn't. I know it looks that way."

"*Looks* that way?" Kate cried. "Christ, Johnny, what do you mean by *that*?"

He picked up the gun again, didn't point it, just held it in the palm of his hand and looked at it, the way a kid looks at a seashell he's picked up on a beach. Still a gun, though. Man's got a gun in a situation like that and laughs, you laugh if you can manage it. At the very least try to smile. He cries, bow your head in respect. He rants, denouncing his enemies both foreign and domestic, sympathize with the fucker.

Above all, try to keep him talking, that's what my old cop friends used to say. You don't want him to jump off that ledge. Long way down. Nice big gun you got there. I know it's loaded, too, because Matt O'Neil showed me. You ready for more snow? More on the way, they say.

"You said it *looks* that way, John. Looks like you killed Mrs. Drexel. Why? Why does it *look* that way?" I asked.

"Because I needed money desperately. The audit will show that. Even the money brokers had become leery of me."

The fire needed work and I decided to take a chance. I got up slowly, walked over, poked it and threw on three new logs. No sudden moves. I had potential weapons in my hands, the poker, the logs. Take a go at him? I could take him, but not with Kate sitting there, I decided. The fire caught and I sat on the couch again.

"I've had it," Johnny said.

"You were over there that night, weren't you? At Mrs. Drexel's."

"Yes, I was." He said it without hesitation. "But she was dead when I arrived."

"Do you know who killed her?"

"Absolutely no idea. And believe me I've thought about it."

"Why did you go there that night?"

"To ask her for money. I was trying to save the bank."

"Can you fill me in on the details?"

"You know anything you tell him he's going to put in the paper," Kate said.

"I don't think that matters much now, Katey. I really don't mind talking about it. It hasn't been very easy living with it. *Boy.*"

"Sarah doesn't know?"

"Not a thing, Kate. I'd never involve her." He closed his eyes and thought for a moment. "Jane dropped by the bank that morning to get some spending money. I cashed a thousand-dollar check for her."

"Why didn't you talk to her then?"

"I thought I'd struck a deal with a New York City money broker for a deposit of a million and a half in hundred-thousand-dollar units. I could have just about made it with that. But the deal fell through later that afternoon. Word gets around."

"So you had the feds breathing down your neck, threatening to close your bank, and nobody left to turn to but Jane Drexel."

"Yes. Exactly. Desperate."

"Did you phone ahead and tell her you were coming to see her?"

"No. You didn't know her, Mac. She would have wanted

to know why." I saw that Kate nodded in agreement. John stood up and waved the big gun around as if it were a baton. "I just drove out here. She didn't answer the bell when I rang and the inside lights were all on. I tried to look through the window but the curtains were drawn. Then I got worried about her, afraid she might have fallen or something. So I let myself in."

"How'd you do that?"

"Jane had combination locks. You punch the right numbers and the lock opens. Except she was always forgetting the combination."

"Noah knew that also," I said. "That's how he let himself in the house to take a look around the morning I found the body."

"Yes, Noah knew it. She'd call him when she forgot. Or she would call me. She kept a copy of the combination with me at the bank. I told her so often I memorized it. Not that it was all that difficult. Four two three one."

"One of the very first sequences any two-bit burglar would have tried."

"That thought occurred to me. The place was a mess inside. I ran through the house looking for Jane, calling her name."

"Didn't you worry that the killer might still be there?"

"I suppose I should have. But I was frantic. Jane meant a lot to me, Mac. I loved her."

"Okay. You couldn't find her in the house so you decided to look outside. Found her body, got scared and ran, right? Well, take it out and try to sell it on the streets and see what you'd get for it. Go pick your twelve closest friends. No, better still, take the guys with the twelve biggest outstanding loans at your bank and put them on the jury. Not even to them could you sell that story. You damn fool."

"That's enough," Kate said. "You're not the law."

"And lucky for him I'm not. Noah knows about the ten thousand dollars, John."

"I am getting confused," Kate said.

"That personal check Jane cashed at the bank wasn't for one thousand, the way you said, Johnny. It was for ten. Big bills. The bank records are going to show that."

"Will somebody please explain to me what you're talking about," Kate said.

"Explain it to Kate exactly the way you'll explain it to a jury, John."

I guess I took it too far. Hell, I know I did because John started crying. No big emotional breakthrough on his part, he just started crying quietly, looking straight ahead, not at either of us but, I suppose, at himself somewhere out there. Depths, distances, dimension, the future forged to the past. He didn't like what he saw.

"I let myself in, just as I said," he told us, wiping his eyes. "And I found poor Jane there, lying on the floor in the living room. Before the fireplace. I felt her pulse, listened for a heartbeat. Nothing. She was dead. I swear to God. I didn't kill her, Kate."

"John, the prosecuting attorney is going to tell the jury you went to borrow money from her and when she turned you down you lost your temper and killed her," I said.

"Damn it, Mac. Can't you see the shape he's in?" Kate said.

"When you found her body you immediately assumed she had been murdered, didn't you. Why? She could have died from a stroke. Or a heart attack, for all you knew at that point."

"No. There were signs of a struggle. Not a fight but a struggle. There was broken glass. The coffee table was tipped on its side. And especially the way Jane looked, lying on her back, face up, eyes open. Anybody would know she had been killed."

"So you dragged her body outside to the patio, then went back and trashed the house." I was guessing.

"Yes, I did."

"Which I don't understand, Johnny. Why did you do that? You should have picked up the phone right then and called Noah. 'Hey, the old lady's dead and I think somebody killed her. You better get over here.' "

"That's what I should have done. I know that now. I just came apart. I thought I could make it look as if some stranger had done it. I was running out of time at the bank. And I'd already run out of money. That's why I went to see her that night."

"To ask her for money?"

"She was my last resort, Mac. I had decided to tell her the absolute truth about everything. And, yes, to ask her to deposit three million more into her account. I could have made it with that."

"And instead of a live pigeon you walked in and found a corpse." A cheap shot, I know. Cheap and vulgar. But didn't he deserve it?

"I was terrified. I knew that once the F.D.I.C. took over, their audit would reveal that I'd transferred money from Jane's account to finance the purchase of the Hollings property. And that would tie me to the murder."

"So you tried to cover up a murder you didn't commit."

"I know it sounds crazy."

"Crazy and dumb. Noah Simmons didn't buy the idea of a stranger as the killer, not for a minute."

"I realize that now."

"And when you trashed the house you found the money."

"It was weird. When Jane came to the bank to cash her check she asked for ten thousand in five-hundred-dollar bills. I just barely came up with it. That's how low my cash supply was."

"You came across the money in the refrigerator, didn't you?"

How could I have know that? John never bothered to ask. He wanted to tell his story.

"I decided to throw all the food out to add to the general confusion I was trying to create. And when I opened the door, there it was."

"What was *it*, exactly?"

"A square baking dish. It was filled with Jell-O. Orange Jell-O."

"Jane was a nut about it," Kate said. "She said it was made out of cows' hooves and had all sorts of things in it that were good for you. She made Jell-O all the time."

"The bills had been rolled up tightly and stuck in the Jell-O. Like birthday candles."

"You took it."

"Of course I took it. The real killer would have if he'd found it, right?"

"I just hope for your sake you didn't put it in your personal checking account."

"I'm not a thief, Mac. I put it back in Jane's account at the bank."

I believed him, believed every word of it. "Well, don't make it any worse than it already is," I said. "Pick up that phone and call Noah. Right now."

"*Boy*. I guess the fellow who said 'Pride goeth before a fall' sure knew what he was talking about, didn't he."

"John, there's a dead man in your bank parking lot. Call Noah. Also, I don't look at you that way."

"Oh, it *was* pride. I admit I stood to make a nice profit from developing this piece of property. But nothing big, nothing that a person in my situation shouldn't be getting. And I put my home up as collateral, remember that."

"You did what you did out of love, Johnny, not pride," Kate said. For the first time since we'd met she was annoying me.

"Love. They say you can't buy love, that love is the one thing money can't buy," John Norton cried. "And they're wrong. If you're a banker and you have money to lend, you can buy love. Believe me. *Boy*."

"You were trying to help people. That's all I'm saying."

"It was my dream to have that bank grow with the Cape and be known as the bank willing to give the good guy a hand. The locals."

"I know, honey."

Honey?

"I wanted all of you to be so proud of me, to know you could depend on me. Which is what I mean by pride going before a fall, Kate."

"Oh, baby, don't be so hard on yourself."

Baby?

"Don't you understand, Kate? I've failed the people here who believed in me. Instead of helping them I've hurt them."

"John knows the feds are going to start calling in all the loans he made," I said. "They'll try to get back as much of the money they pay out in insurance as they can."

"The chamber of commerce was going to name me Man of the Year. It's supposed to be a secret but I knew. How can I face any of them again?"

"Hundreds of banks in this country are going under right now," I said. "You're not exactly alone. Lots of company."

"They say misery loves company."

"I'm not saying you don't have problems. But you're still a young man and it's not the end of the world for you."

"I've had it, Mac. You know that. I'll go to jail."

That was all Kate needed. She put her hands over her face and started sobbing.

"You're the girl I should have married," he told her.

"Please don't say that. Please don't," she managed to say.

I prayed silently he would shut up. No such luck. He was falling from the sky like an angel with his wings on fire. A tragic figure? Within the warped and distorted framework of today's life, with its confusing and conflicting rules of conduct and deportment, I suppose he was, in his way.

"Dumb," he said to Kate. "You're Catholic. Isn't that absurd? My mother certainly didn't approve when we went together that summer. And did she let me know it! *Boy.*"

Enough. "Do me a big favor," I said. "Get the fuck out of here, Johnny. And take that gun and all your troubles with you. Go on now. Leave us the hell alone."

He stood up. "You're right, Mac. I'm going. It's not fair to burden you with my problems. I'm sorry. But I wanted Kate to understand." Ever the gent, he was.

"Johnny, I'm going with you!" Kate tried to get up but I pulled her back.

"Keep her here, Mac."

"Johnny, don't leave."

"I've got a lot of things to think about, a lot of decisions to make," John said, as much to himself as to us. He walked toward the door, gun in hand. And I held on to Kate, which was not easy, held on grimly with arms wrapped around her while she kicked and clawed, screamed and scratched and tried to bite me. You see, I was holding on to my life. For whatever it was worth.

"Don't let him! Don't you let him!" she screamed.

Johnny walked out the door without looking back.

"Let me go, please let me go," she pleaded.

"For God's sake, he's out of his mind and he's got a loaded gun in his hands. He could kill you."

"He's going to kill himself. I can stop him. Let me go!"

We were fighting on the couch. "He's not going to kill you, too."

"I hate you!"

"I love you, Kate. Please."

In her panic, she ignored my plea. "Johnny, please come back. Please, please come back to me!" she cried.

I don't know if he heard her screams or not. He walked out without closing the door behind him, the way people will when they have things on their mind. I don't know if he heard her. I don't think he was listening.

There was then a sudden glare and a sweep of bright lights through the front windows and the open door, a car sliding into the driveway. There were shouts, the sweep of a searchlight, and moments later Bascombe Midgeley came crashing into the living room with a look of panic on his face.

"Where is he? Where's Johnny?"

"He just walked out that door," I said to him.

"His car's still outside. Noah's looking around the grounds. Christ, what a mess."

"Bascombe, he's got a gun and he's in bad shape. Be careful." I had my arms locked around Kate.

Bascombe turned and ran out the door, shouting into the dark, "Johnny? You crazy son of a bitch! It's me, Bascombe!"

That was when John Norton, handsome and widely admired young Cape Cod banking president, beloved husband of plain, barren but kindly Sarah, small-town achiever who dreamed the American dream and never meant to harm anybody, shot and killed himself. When Kate and I heard the shot she immediately ceased struggling with me. I let go of her and we sat there on the couch. Neither of us made a move to go outside because the sound of the gunshot had been so final.

I told her I was going to call an ambulance. She told me she hated me. I called the ambulance, then called the North Walpole police station and told the dispatcher to send the paramedic squad. Kate told me I was a coward. I don't remember all the things she called me. Everything she could think of. I quit listening after a while, to tell the truth.

The paramedics got there first. There was no need for any ambulance, no need for a doctor or any emergency equipment, no need for anything except a body bag and a meat wagon with snow tires.

John had walked through the snow and sleet from the house down to the shore of the pond. I think he probably just wandered down there, going where his feet led him. He did his business with his back to the pond so the impact from the bullet he put through the roof of his mouth and his brain sent his body falling into the water. A neat job.

Kate sat on the couch with MouMou in her lap and cursed me while I kept my mouth shut and took it. She quietly cursed, damned and condemned me and ground my heart to powder, Kate did.

After they hauled the body away Bascombe came back, wet, cold and coatless. Kate jumped up and ran and they embraced. "I covered him," he told her. "You don't have to worry about that. Noah and I pulled him out of the water and I covered him with my coat."

Noah came inside then, filled the room, dripping wet and breathing hard. Without a word he walked over and folded the both of them into his huge, outstretched arms, and the three of them stood there, rocking and swaying, crying and mourning together.

I wanted to join them because I loved all of them and I wanted to share their grief. But young people mourning the death of one of their own need special privacy. So I kept away. I knew my place.

This old-timer kept out of it, went to the kitchen and poured himself half a glass of raw vodka and gulped it down. Then this old war-horse went and flopped into the same chair where the late Johnny had sat. I picked up the telephone and called the Boston *Globe*.

Never missed a deadline in my life.

FIFTEEN

"**M**Y, DON'T WE LOOK NICE," I said when Noah Simmons opened his front door. He was wearing jeans and a sweatshirt and he had a red-and-white checked apron tied around his waist.

"Come on in." He led me through the house to the kitchen where a big black cast-iron kettle sat on the stove, steam leaking from its lid. "I'm making a little chowder. It'll be ready in a few minutes if you're interested."

"I'm interested. Here. I brought you something. The sour mash is for Dede. The framboise liqueur is for you. Try it on vanilla ice cream."

"Dede's in Hyannis with the kids shopping for spring clothes at Sears. I shall tell her of your thoughtful gesture."

It was early Saturday afternoon, another raw, gray day and I had dropped by to visit with Noah without calling ahead. A week had passed since John Norton's death. I hadn't gone to the funeral. Enough's enough.

"It's a good-bye present," I told Noah. "I'm going to Beantown. Taking a full-time job on the *Globe*."

"Are you now? Kate know about this?"

"No, not yet."

"We were getting used to you around here."

"It's not all that far away."

"Yes, it is. I bet I don't get there twice a year."

"What choice have I got? I need a job and they're offering me one. I can't turn it down. Fifty and counting and you find you need a little security. I'm going to be taking off sometime tomorrow."

"Well, I wish you luck. Boston's a good town. If you like big cities. Which I don't." He took the lid off the kettle and used a wooden spoon to test his chowder. "Not quite. Give it five more minutes. Potatoes need it."

"It smells good but it looks like dirty dishwater."

"Which is the way real clam chowder should look. I hate the way most restaurants make it, thick and white as a Tastee-Freeze. You should use milk, not cream. Salt pork, never bacon. Not too much onion. And quahogs, the bigger the better. Slice them up. Adds to the taste. That is Simmons-family clam chowder, my friend, the way we've been making it for ever since I can remember."

"Kate won't have anything to do with me, Noah."

He opened two cans of beer and handed one to me. "Mac, I've tried to talk to her. She won't listen to reason. You did exactly what you should have done that night. I've told her that. You were dealing with a man in a state of shock who had a gun in his hand."

"He was rocky as hell. I could have taken him easily except with Kate there I just couldn't take the chance."

"You did the right thing. I'll say it again."

"I feel a little guilty about it, I guess is what I'm trying to say. If I'd taken him he'd be alive today."

"And if you'd tried and failed, you and Kate might both be dead."

"She thinks if I had let her go after him she could have made him come to his senses."

"Kate is Kate, Mac. Will of iron. At times. Gets her mind set it's hard to change it. You were trying to protect her, which is what you should have done."

"I believed Johnny when he told us he didn't kill Jane Drexel. I believe everything he said."

"He was telling you the truth. Johnny didn't kill anybody. Except himself. O'Neil's death was strictly an accident."

"I had it in my mind that maybe it was O'Neil who killed Jane."

"Because he'd bought the Hollings place with the loan he got from John, I know. It makes sense. Somehow Jane learned about it and threatened to blow the whole thing apart. And wouldn't that make it nice and easy for everybody, him being dead and all. The problem is he was in New Bedford that night with his girlfriend. There's a seafood place they hung out at there. I got three witnesses who saw them that night at the bar."

"Then you've still got an unsolved murder on your hands."

Noah stirred the chowder one final time and turned off the flame. "We'll let it sit for a minute, gather its forces."

"There's only one person left then. It's got to be the old man. I can't believe it, but it has to be. He told me he wasn't at Jane Drexel's house that night. He said they talked over the phone the previous afternoon and were planning to have lunch together the day I found her body."

Noah ladled the chowder into two big bowls. "I didn't tell you about the supper dishes. Johnny did a good job of trashing the house. But for some reason he didn't touch the dining-room table. Where two people had eaten supper, fish chowder to be exact, and left the dirty dishes for the maid to clear the next day. Also, there was broken glass around the fireplace and tests showed somebody had been drinking Kahlúa."

"So she calls and invites him to supper. They eat, then go sit before the fire. She tells him she's giving him ten thousand dollars. Except it's in frozen assets. He said that's what she told him. A mystery he must solve. She loved mysteries and she loved taunting him. Who's desperate for money."

"You see, I think she was planning to give him the money before he left for home that night, serve it as a late dessert maybe," Noah said. "Remember, she had it rolled up like candles and stuck in a bowl of Jell-O in the refrigerator."

" 'Frozen assets. Don't you think that is amusing, Gerald?' " I mimicked.

"Teasing him as usual."

"Rubbing his nose in it as usual," I said. "So he tries playing the game, but gets nowhere. She's enjoying it. Needless to say, he's not. And finally he loses his temper, just snaps. After thirty years. And I'll tell you something else, Noah. I think he knew she hadn't forgotten where the money was and also knew she would end up giving it to him before the night was over. He didn't kill her trying to make her tell. He did it because the humiliation was too much to bear. After thirty years he finds himself with his hands around her throat. And couldn't let go."

Noah nodded. He didn't want to look at me.

"Is that what you've thought all along?" I asked.

"It's what I hoped all along wouldn't turn out to be the case."

"You planning on taking it to a grand jury?"

"Do you think I'd get an indictment?"

"No, probably not. But he didn't clean up after himself very well that night, did he?"

"He killed her and ran. I think he was horrified by what he did. He's not a violent person by nature. Gentle as a lamb."

We ate his superb chowder and drank his Rolling Rock beer in silence. I still knew something he didn't know. Should I tell him about Kate's mother's confession, that there was a very good chance that Gerald Dickerson and Jane Drexel were Kate's father and mother?

Should I tell him I had concluded that Jane Drexel could not bring herself to tell Kate the truth, but also couldn't bear the thought of not providing for her, at least indirectly? Her only child, after all, and as spoiled and self-centered as Jane was, that was important, especially as she had grown older. So she had rigged everything, the summer school, a quality education for all four of them, the trust, everything.

No, I decided. I would trust Noah Simmons with my life, but this was between Kate and me. One day maybe I would tell her. And if Father Terry Riley after too many pops proved to be a gossip then he would hear from me.

Noah finished his beer and crushed the can in his hand. "What can I do? What would you do? He's almost eighty. He won't be around for much longer."

"I've written my last word on the subject, if that's what you're getting at. But we're talking about first-degree murder."

"You want to see him in jail? Make sure he doesn't go free to kill again? Who's he going to kill?"

"I know it's a tough call, Noah."

"Jane was tough on him. People think passions dry up in old people. In some they do, but not all. For that matter, most old people don't think of themselves as being old."

"You're saying it's not worth the trouble to try to bring him to trial. You're also saying it was a crime of passion."

"It's like when the family dog goes for the baby's face because the baby poked him in the eye once too often. Ten seconds later the baby is being rushed to the emergency room and the dog is hiding in a corner, quivering and whining, is what I'm saying."

"I'd destroy the dog."

"Oh, to hell with you. You know what I mean."

"Yes. So what are you going to do?"

"Keep him on a very short leash, that's what. That's what I've decided." And clearly he was miserable with the decision.

"Over your garage door. You've got the bow name of the old Cape Cod boat. *Justice*."

"It was a birthday present from Dede."

"Well, I guess somebody has to administer it. As best they can."

"We've had enough excitement here for one winter. I want to get this town quieted down, damn it." He looked out his kitchen window. "Christ, he taught me Latin. He's old and he's blind as a bat. Old people just give out on you, up one day and down the next. I wouldn't be surprised to see him in a nursing home a year from now, maybe sooner. Not worth the trouble."

"You love him, don't you?"

"I guess. Yes, I do." He refilled our chowder. *"Haec res completa. Facta est. Edemus nunc et bibemus, amice care!"*

SIXTEEN

I FOUND BASCOMBE MIDGELEY at work in his office and looking sharp in tan pleated corduroys, a blue chamois shirt and bright red suspenders. He also looked tired and harassed and I told him so.

"I've got my hands full, old cock," he said. "Up to my neck in work on the trust and, of course, I'm Johnny's lawyer and I've got his estate to settle. Not to mention all the bank business." He grinned. "Actually, I'm making a little money out of all this."

"Is Sarah going to be okay?"

"Johnny didn't leave her a lot of money. He told you the truth when he said he hadn't been robbing the bank blind. And as it turns out, he and Sarah were living up to the hilt, just like the rest of us."

"What about the loan for two hundred thousand he made to himself?"

"There's no problem there. The North Walpole Trust is buying the Hollings estate, assuming both loans. The bank examiners have already agreed to it. Happy to get the money back, in fact. And that also lets Matt O'Neil's wife off the hook. Remember, Mac, despite what you may hear to the contrary, money *can* buy happiness. Much of the time."

"So Sarah gets to keep the house."

"She does. That's about all, but it's worth maybe three hundred and change on today's market. Not bad."

Bascombe removed his eyeglasses and massaged the bridge of his nose. "Sarah informs me that she plans to sell the house and move to, ah, San Francisco, I believe it is. Fresh start. After all, she's young and there are no children. I am encouraging her to do so."

"What about all those orphans they've adopted?"

"All those orphans are now wards of the trust. Kate has been a mover and shaker, let me tell you. It won't cost that much to support them, after all. Little Third-Worlders. Live on rice and fish heads." Bascombe chuckled at his joke.

"What's Sarah going to do in San Francisco, does she know?"

"Find herself? Something like that. Hell, I don't know, Mac. Isn't that why young widows and divorcees go to San Francisco? And with the hundred and fifty thousand or so she'll get out of the house, she'll have plenty of time to go about it, won't she?"

"How is she upstairs?"

"Shattered. What you'd expect. She adored Johnny and she had no idea of the trouble he was in. He kept it all to himself. So it was like being one of the astronauts' wives when the space shuttle exploded."

"What made him do it, Bascombe? He must have known he was digging himself a hole."

"I've thought about it, believe me, old cock. I've stayed awake nights and thought about it. I think it was because, except for this one time, things had always worked out for the best for him. He took success for granted."

"That's what cynics say about our country."

"I'm serious, old cock. Johnny had never failed at anything. *Never*. Success came so easily to him. And nobody

213

who knew him ever dreamed that John Norton ever would fail at anything. He was always so confident, so optimistic."

"He told me it was a matter of too much pride, which goes before a fall."

"I remember once in high school we were thirteen points behind Orleans with three minutes to play in the game. You know what Johnny said to us in the huddle? Now here's how we're going to win this son of a bitch."

"And you did win."

"And we did."

"He was so frantic and despondent that last night. Haunted. Sentimental. Almost maudlin. Feeling sorry for himself."

"Because failure was a totally new experience for him. He didn't know how to handle it, the way most of us do who win a few, lose a few, see a few get rained out."

"What bank business are you involved in?"

"I've been negotiating with the examiners. They're not bad guys, just doing a job. I've got five new clients who're trying to cut deals on their loans."

"Johnny didn't play by the rules, Bascombe."

"That's true, but the rules in banking have been completely rewritten. Since interest rates were deregulated it's become a competitive business. Everybody's into banking today, including Sears, Roebuck."

"And the competition was simply too much for him?"

"He got himself overextended trying to be all things for all people here on the Cape. Consumer loans. Personal loans. Commercial loans. Real estate development loans. Ten-year loans when he should have limited them to five years max. You should hear Bob Hertgen on the subject."

"A lot of bad loans?"

"A few. Any banker will make a few bad loans he'll have to swallow. But some of Johnny's loans eventually will turn over."

"And if Jane hadn't been killed and he could have persuaded her to deposit three million more in the bank?"

"He probably would have made it. Just one more step and he would have caught the ball. A diving catch, but he would have made it."

"The North Walpole Trust lost a bundle, didn't it?"

"A big one. Poor Johnny. He didn't mean for that to happen."

"It still didn't mean he had to kill himself."

Bascombe ran his fingers through his hair, replaced his glasses and shook his head. "I don't know. I've thought about it. Maybe if you were Johnny you had to."

"I'm moving to Boston, Bascombe."

"What? And miss all the fun of seeing spring arrive on the Cape? Surely you know that after only two or three more miserable months of cloudy, chilly weather, one day the first sprig of green will be sighted somewhere between here and Truro. And after that, it's only a matter of time, another six weeks or so, and you can go outside and be fairly comfortable without an overcoat. You owe it to yourself to stick around for it."

"I've just come from a talk with Noah."

"I'm told you enjoyed his clam chowder. Best on the Cape. Hell, best in all of New England."

"He called you?"

"The minute you left his house. Don't be a fool, McFarland. We're trying very hard to make you part of us here. Don't you know that? We don't do it often and, frankly, we don't like to be rebuffed, old cock. So just go on to Boston and win yourself some of those many prizes you people so enjoy passing out to yourselves. If that is your determination."

I looked out at the main street of North Walpole, not a bad view from Bascombe's second-floor office window. "I like it here. A lot."

"We're not that much different from the rest of the country, you know. It does take a little more time to accept new people. After all, we were isolated here for so very long. But you're welcome, Mac. We wish you'd stay and become one of us."

"I don't think Kate feels that way."

"Has she given you permission to leave?"

"Very funny. Whose side are you on?"

He thought about it. "Yours. Noah and I certainly don't think you can handle her. Nobody can do that. We do think you may be able to *contain* her. To some degree. And make her happy, old cock."

"She won't give me the time of day."

He looked at his watch. "A little after three. Be at the Binnacle at five. I'll give her a call."

I turned to leave. "A short leash," I said, couldn't help myself. "That's what Noah said he was going to do with the old man?"

There was a moment's silence. My back was to Bascombe.

"There's a prolonged problem any other way," he said. "With a messy trial and far too much publicity. Better to just let it fade away, become the subject of tales to be told and retold long after all of us are gone. Binnacle gossip. A story they'll tell at Bob's."

"I gather this was a group decision. A group I'm being invited to join."

"Mac, the old man's trying very hard to forget it ever happened. And by and large I think he's succeeded. Leave it alone! Please!"

"Bascombe, I'm going for a ride, take a look around. It's really a very pretty little town." I walked out of his office, through his secretary's office and headed down the stairs.

"Especially if you want to stay out here with us," Bascombe called after me. "Leave it alone!"

216

"No. I'm going to see him. There are things I have to decide for myself." I was thinking about Kate, of course.

"Leave it alone!" The door to the street closed behind me.

SEVENTEEN

GERALD DICKERSON OPENED his front door and squinted at me. "Why, what a most pleasant surprise. Who is it?" he called.

"It's me. McFarland."

"Mac! I heard your automobile horn and I didn't know who it could possibly be."

"Yeah. Well, it's me all right." I was trying my best to sound tough, stern and mean and tough, but it wasn't coming out right. I hadn't even got out of my rented car, just pulled into the driveway and sat on the horn until he came to the door.

"I'm sorry I failed to recognize you, Mac," the old man said. "I've misplaced my very last pair of glasses, I'm afraid. So you'll have to bear with me. Care to come inside? It's raw out here."

"No. Walk out here to the car. I want a few words with you, my friend," said this really tough person.

"Very well, Mac. I shall try." He felt his way down the steps, both hands on the iron railing. "Mac, would you mind very much giving me a countdown so I can home in on you? Ten, nine, eight, and so forth?"

I kid you not. Can't you picture the two of us? Absurd. He stumbled across the pebbled driveway, hands out as if he were playing blindman's buff, while I counted. Mean guy.

"Stop right there," I ordered when he was four or five feet from the car. Jesus, I should have known.

Despite the clear warning Noah had tried to give me, Gerald Dickerson's general appearance was startling. The ruddy glow of good health was gone from his face and it seemed to me he had lost a lot of weight, not that he weighed that much to begin with. He looked suddenly frail, his complexion was chalky white, and his hands trembled slightly. His new lamb's-wool sweater sloped over his thin shoulders. Noah was right. People as old as he can turn the corner overnight.

I had come, what? To warn him, admonish him? "They know," I said, a good no-nonsense start.

"How nice for them." He was trying to stand at attention, chin up, hands at his sides, staring at the radio antenna.

"You know what I'm saying."

"Sorry, Mac. Would you repeat that?"

"Move a little closer to the car."

"Oh! Sorry!" He edged forward as if he were approaching the rim of a live volcano. "You see, I could not find my glasses." He would have walked right into the side of the car except that I held up my arm, palm out, and stopped him.

"Oh! Here we are. Thanks, Mac. You see, I was lying on the couch taking a rest when I heard your horn. I couldn't imagine who in the world it could be. To tell the truth, I can't remember when anyone has ever pulled into this driveway before and blown his horn, so you can see why I was puzzled. I made it out to Jane's grave this morning and it tired me out, took the wind right out of my sails, let me tell you. But when you're eighty . . . next month.

I'm trying to get out there at least twice a week, weather permitting." He paused and thought, still looking at the antenna. "For the very life of me! Getting as bad as Jane, I am. What was it I was saying, Mac?"

"Your glasses."

"What about them? Oh, you found them, did you? Good."

"No, no. You misplaced them."

"I did? Oh, of course I did. No problem. Nice of you to remind me, however. They're bound to be in there some-place. It's simply a matter of patting and feeling around in the immediate area until I come across them. Nothing for you to worry your head about. You never found those I lost in your yard, by chance? I would love to have them back, should you come across them."

"They all still seem to love you, which frankly I find hard to believe."

"I see. At least I think I do. I'm almost certain I do, in fact. How nice for them. Mac, you didn't come across my glasses by any chance, did you?"

I tried but I found it impossible to imagine how it had been that snowy night when, at long last, and for one more petty reason, a rage, a bitter anger which had been roiling inside him for decades, suddenly overwhelmed him.

A rage, I decided, sparked by shame, perhaps, and maybe an old shame remembered. Shame for loving her still, de-spite the indignities she had forced him to accept. Shame because of his financial dependence on her. She had made him stand on his hind legs and do tricks for so many years, entreat her, before she tossed him his doggy biscuits. Crisp, flat bills tucked inside a volume of Ovid's poetry, tightly rolled bills stuck in Jell-O. So amusing, and he was required to act surprised and pleased, grin and say thank you. Shame.

Poked by the baby-lady in the eye once too often, his attack couldn't have lasted more than a few moments that night, so old and so frail both of them were. But that had been long enough.

I didn't know what to say to him.

"Well, Mac, what have you got to say for yourself?" he asked cheerfully. "Just stopped by to say hello, did you? Always good to see you."

"You just watch your step," I said.

"Oh, indeed I shall. A person my age. These old bones are brittle, I am most aware of that. One fall, one misstep could put me out of commission. Break my hip. But so far, so good. Dear Kate drove me down to Hyannis two days ago, in fact, for a look-see at Cape Cod Hospital. So far, so good, as they say."

"Well, take care of yourself." I couldn't believe I said it.

"I will tell you this. Every night I go to sleep thinking about Jane. Not a night passes when I don't think about her. Kahlúa and milk. And some nights I wake up and my heart is beating a mile a minute. It feels like a bird's wings fluttering inside me. But I have found if I have a little Kahlúa in a glass of milk it goes away. I say to myself, 'Well, Jane, the bird is perched. He's resting. His wings have stopped fluttering.' So far, so good. Which is exactly what I told the fellow at Cape Cod Hospital. Besides, my hospital insurance isn't worth sneezing at. So I will certainly watch my step. You don't have to worry about that for one minute, Mac."

I started the car, then thought better of it, turned off the engine, opened the door and, taking him by the arm, guided Mr. Dickerson back to the front door of his house. Offered to help find his glasses but he said he'd rather conduct the search himself because it was a challenge, it gave him something to do, and it taught him to be more careful and think ahead next time he took them off.

"And I will be seeing you around, young man," he said, swinging his arm, trying to give me a jolly slap on the shoulder. Missed by a good six inches.

Short leash. He didn't need a leash at all. Leave it alone. Bascombe was right.

EIGHTEEN

KATE MADE ME COOL MY HEELS for the better part of an hour before she finally appeared at the Binnacle that afternoon, looked around until she spotted me at the table beside the fireplace, strode over, very businesslike, and sat down. "I really can't stay very long," she said. "I had to make the time to come here."

"Would you like a drink?"

"Oh, no, thanks. I've still got lots of work to do tonight so I don't think I'd better have a drink with you. Frankly, you drink too much, Mac."

Nice start, perfect lift-off, all systems go.

Kate had fixed herself up, makeup, contacts, high-heel shoes, hair washed and blown dry, red wool jersey dress, and a black mink coat, latest style, which obviously had been expropriated from one of Jane Drexel's closets. *Haut* Cape. Also, I thought she'd had a couple of drinks somewhere because her cheeks were flushed.

"Working tonight, Saturday night? Things must be jumping," I said.

"We're moving into Jane's house Monday morning, lock, stock and barrel. Everything in the office is lying on the floor, as you can imagine. What a mess."

"It sounds like you're really getting down to business."

"What's that supposed to be, a sarcastic remark, or what?"

"No."

"Well, what did you mean?"

"I was just wondering how things were going, that's all."

"It's not fair to expect me to become an actual expert overnight, Mac. There's a lot of money involved and a lot of things that need to be done. One step at a time, that's how I intend to handle it."

"Which I think is wise of you."

"Which is exactly what somebody like you would say. I know you think I don't know anything, which you're totally wrong about, by the way."

"Kate, I didn't say you don't know anything. Please don't put words in my mouth."

"I need expert advice, which is exactly what I intend to get before I spend a penny of that money."

"This is a beautiful place here, Kate. And you've been given a great opportunity to keep it that way. Just to accomplish that will be a big challenge. You can't save the whole Cape. You might be able to save North Walpole, though."

"Don't preach to me." She crossed her legs. Jesus, what legs. Her eyes were purple, then she would move her head a bit one way or the other and they were blue, then green. "You just love to preach to people." Her hair gold, then white.

Change the subject. "I saw Mr. Dickerson. Dropped by. He didn't look too good."

"He has Alzheimer's disease, the early stages of it. I took him to Hyannis a couple of days ago for a checkup because I suspected it."

"Do Noah and Bascombe know about this?" She nodded, which cleared up a lot of things. "What do you plan to do about him?"

"Let him make it on his own for as long as he can, and

he's doing okay right now. But we'll take care of him. When he needs help, he'll have it."

It is called taking care of your own, except that Kate didn't know that was what she was doing, and, furthermore, using Jane Drexel's money to do it, perhaps by instinct. Certainly, in its propriety, there was a great ironic justice to it all; the dutiful daughter seeing after ailing father and using dear, departed mother's money to pay the bills. The system works!

I knew then I would never tell Kate what I knew about the past, about Jane and Gerald, star-crossed lovers, and I would urge Father Terry Riley to close the book on the subject as well. It was none of our business, after all. It was Kate's business and she was taking care of it very well.

Mary Beth appeared, all tits in faded jeans and a black T-shirt which said across its chest ALL THIS & BRAINS TOO. "Happy hour has officially begun," she told us.

"Mary Beth, excuse me, but you've put on a little weight," I said.

"I know. I been back on the fucking rabbit food for a week now and the scales won't move."

I told her to bring me another beer and a vodka on the rocks for Kate, who didn't protest.

"You really like her type, don't you?" she said.

"Will you get off my back? I wanted a chance to tell you how sorry I am about Johnny. I know what he meant to you. I truly liked him, Kate, and I'm sorry you feel the way you do about me."

"Mac, I owe you an apology for the way I acted. And for what I said. And I should have said it sooner. I owe you that."

"You don't owe me anything."

Mary Beth brought our drinks. Kate took a slug of hers. "Boston, huh?" she said.

"I'm driving up tomorrow."

"They hired you? Honest to God?"

"I start Monday."

"That is simply wonderful, Mac. I'm so happy for you. It's a great chance to rebuild your life. Especially at your age."

"I don't know much about Boston. Never even been there."

"Oh, you'll learn. In a hurry. You're a quick study, Mac. And I've always thought small-town life isn't for you. You're strictly a big-city type person. You thrive best in a big city. With bars where you can go and drink with other big-city types. We're just hicks out here on the Cape."

"I guess." Couldn't resist it.

"Maybe a story will bring you down this way sometime. I doubt it, though. Nothing much ever happens here. But, Mac, you simply must buy yourself some new clothes. Boston is a snappy town with snappy dressers and you are going to look like a bum in those clothes you walk around in. How long has it been since you bought yourself a new jacket? Please believe me on that one, is all I can say."

"I'll raid Brooks Brothers the moment I can afford it."

"I'll tell you one other thing. If you go there and try to live the way you were when I found you, like a pig, drinking far too much and not eating right and feeling sorry for yourself, I guarantee you're going to fall flat on your ass. I mean, it's none of my business but you mark my words."

"I'm all over that. Thanks to you."

"You're getting on, do you know that? A few more years and you'll be drawing Social Security."

"Kate, I'm only fifty."

"Exactly. Also, you're not Catholic. I've thought a lot about that. You're not anything that I can tell. I mean, do you actually belong to any sort of regular Christian group?"

"Will you have dinner with me, Kate? It's Saturday night. We could drive down to Hyannis if you like."

"God, no. That would keep you up too late and you've got to drive all the way to Boston tomorrow and get yourself settled in. I'd just as soon eat right here."

"Here? Kate, this is the *Binnacle*."

"Well, it's certainly not fancy like the places in Boston you'll be going to. Let's just forget it. To tell the truth, I'm not even hungry."

"I know you've been through hell. Jane, your mother, Johnny. All the people you loved."

"It hasn't exactly been easy."

"You're right. I'm a big-city guy. I like the action and the feel of a big town. I'm a big-city newspaperman and I always will be, I guess. It's in my blood. I like working in a newspaper city room. My corner of the world. I feel at home in a place where something's going on. Where people come and go. Big buildings. Action. I like to be a part of that. Because I have spent most of my adult life being part of that. You understand?"

"Of course. I understand perfectly. That's what I'm trying to tell you, that I understand, Mac."

"It's the intrigue, Kate. The cops, big-city cops. The crime. The pols on the make, money and power. It just throbs. And as a reporter you're part of it and yet you're not. And you're right, I like to drink and joke and gossip with my friends in a bar after deadline. There is no warmer place in this world than a newspaper bar, Kate. Christ, it's what I *am*."

"I *know* that. Don't you think I know that? For your information, you haven't told me one thing I don't already know."

"There, in my place, I'm somebody. Sure of myself. Two years I'll own Boston. Bust the town wide open. I'm a good reporter, what I like to do best, born to do, I guess. Those bastards in Chicago took it away from me. And now I have a chance to put it together again. It's not easy, believe me."

"I *said* it hasn't been easy. Didn't I say that?"

Mary Beth floated by, bearing a tray filled with drinks. "Just let me know when you're ready for another one," she said.

"I'll have a Scotch on the rocks. A double, I guess. Hell, make it two doubles." It was happy hour. Happy hour at the Binnacle. The only bar open between here and Hyannis. "Do you want another drink, Kate? Anything at all?"

"No. Nothing. I don't want anything from you."

Except the rest of my life.

I sighed. "Okay, just tell me one thing. How in the hell am I going to make a living in a burg like this?"

She glared at me. Her bottom lip was quivering. Only slightly, but it was quivering.

"That's more like it," Kate said.

DOUGLAS KIKER is one of the nation's best known and most widely respected television news correspondents. As a reporter for *The Atlanta Journal*, he observed the turmoil of the Southern civil rights movement. As White House correspondent for the *New York Herald Tribune*, he was present in Dallas when President Kennedy was killed. As an NBC News correspondent, he has covered every national political convention since 1964. He reported for NBC News from Vietnam, Northern Ireland, the Middle East, and, on special assignment, the revolution in Iran. For his reports on the Jordan war, in 1970, he was awarded broadcasting's most coveted prize, the George Foster Peabody Award. He is the author of two novels, *The Southerner* and *Strangers on the Shore*. His articles and short stories have appeared in *The Atlantic Monthly*, *Harper's*, and *The Yale Review* among other publications.